SINGLETON

Singleton decided to loaf away the entire summer so when he fell in with some Arapahoe Indians he enjoyed their aspen-camp and agreed to meet them up in Colorado, but when he got up there, he found them dead—murdered in cold blood. Instead of loafing away the summer, he went searching for the killers, and when he found them down near a cowtown named Fletcherville, he and the town constable from up north, at Cutbank, encountered more trouble than just the renegades made for them.

They also ran into a bad law officer, several very close calls with death, and in the end could hardly wait to get away from the Fletcherville country, and for Singleton, he could hardly wait to get back to loafing, after he had re-earned the right to loaf.

SINGLETON

BADGER CLARK

ST. MARTIN'S PRESS
NEW YORK

ROBERT HALE LIMITED
LONDON

© *Robert Hale Limited 1978*
First published 1978

St. Martin's Press, Inc.,
175 Fifth Avenue
New York, N.Y. 10010

Library of Congress Cataloging in Publication Data

Clark, Badger.
  Singleton.

  I. Title.
PZ4.C5914Si   [PS3553.L267]   813′.5′4   78-2416

ISBN 0 312 72599 X (*regular edition*)
ISBN 0 312 72600 7 (*large print*)

ISBN 0 7091 6776 8 (*regular edition*)
ISBN 0 7091 6775 X (*large print*)

Robert Hale Limited
Clerkenwell House
Clerkenwell Green
London EC1R 0HT

Printed in Great Britain by
Billing & Sons Limited, Guildford, London and Worcester

1

A DIFFERENT LAND

When dawn arrived the entire upland-world rolled back its dark vestiges revealing peaks so lofty they had glaze-ice, like a glacier, and down from those cloud-misted heights the mountains were massive dark-veined granite, until below timber-line. From there down to the foothills there were stands of fir and pine so thick the sun had been unable to reach down through in centuries.

Out across the gentler foothills where the grassland ran southward in gentle undulations, like a pale sea frozen in motion, a man could see in three directions, west, east, and southward, until the farthest curve of skyline bent around far-hazed additional rims and ridges.

Later, after about eleven o'clock in the morning, heat-hazes would arrive to further restrict a man's visibility, but even then by Singleton's best estimate he was able to see several hundred miles, and that was enough for anyone.

He saw little bunches of distant cattle, mostly redbacks, and twice he saw the tan-tawny dust of fleet bands of horses, but all the time he was crossing this vastness he did not see another person. Once, he saw what could have been a distant town; sunrise bouncing off iron roofs which were in a rough cluster, and another time, when he was closer to the foothills on his way towards those awesomely forbidding mountains, he saw the squatty log structures where a cow-outfit was headquartered.

He did not deviate from his direct

approach into the foothills. His need at the present was not for the companionship of a ranch nor the conveniences of a town.

The weather turned warm, but slowly, for despite the fact that this was summertime, at the elevations Singleton had been riding lately a man could expect a rind of frost atop his bedroll every morning when he rolled out.

But there were compensations. Unlike the far southward country where Singleton had come from, in the highlands there was abundant water, stronger feed, and a man never had difficulty finding firewood for his breakfast or supper fires. Also the heat, which got warm enough by mid-morning this time of year—summertime—was different from the desert's bone-dry and dehydrating heat.

The trick, as Singleton saw it, was to become accustomed to the cold mornings and nights in summertime so that, come winter, a man's blood would be able to properly thicken. Otherwise he would have to wear long underwear the year round.

It was also good game country. Singleton had been eating very well since crossing Raton Pass. In fact midway across Colorado he and his horse had both begun to gain a little weight, which was unusual for animals with two or four legs who were constantly moving.

In the fallen-timber country he had received the drifter's inevitable motivation; he had encountered an Arapahoe buck, with his wife and young daughter, and had spent a month in their foothill camp among the aspens and creek-willows helping them 'make meat' from trout and deer. They had had good times in that aspen-camp. They had laughed a lot together, had hunted, had sat almost each night in the red-gold soft blaze of a springtime fire out front of the hide hut to smoke and exchange stories, anecdotes, even philosophies, and the woman, who had been shy for the first two or three weeks, finally had accepted Singleton.

The child had been twelve, near the edge of budding womanhood, with liquid soft dark eyes and hair as dark as the wing of a crow, with bluish lights when the sun struck it just right. Singleton had given her a little oval mirror. He'd been carrying the thing for several years. His personal mirror was a polished piece of oblong steel—a heliograph mirror, in fact, a reminder of earlier times when Singleton had served the army.

The girl's name had been Lupin, named probably for the first thing her mother had seen after delivery, which was common practice, and she had always been shy with Singleton, but smiling-shy.

She had used her eyes, and her smile, to flirt. Singleton had been flattered and touched. Her father said one night at their fire after the women had retired, that he had seen littler girls, six and seven years old, do that. Singleton had smiled.

"They are born with the knowledge, friend. They are women and they are born with all the secrets of their kind."

The buck had tamped his pipe before responding. He had seldom made a solemn comment without thought. Now, he said, "Maybe no one ever knows what is right, but I don't want her to pair up with anyone but another Arapahoe." He raised black eyes. "We are men together and we can speak together. You understand?"

It was the third week of their association. They could indeed speak together. Singleton nodded solemnly. "I understand. But the land is filling up. Do you know how to keep her among her own kind for the next three or four years?"

"I know how," replied the hunter, and leaned closer to the firelight to begin a sketch in the dust with a rigid forefinger. "This is here, where we are now. The aspen-camp. Here—this is the low trail to the highlands. Beyond the Absaroka of the Crows, beyond the Sioux's Sand Hills, into the country of Tall Timber and White Winter. You see; this is the trail to the mountains called Tara." The Indian looked up. "Beyond your Great Divide onto the Big Sky Plains."

Singleton said, "Montana. Through those Taras?"

The Indian smiled slowly. "No. Into them though." He made a sweeping big gesture with outflung arms. "Big. Hundreds of miles through. Hundreds and hundreds." He dropped his arms and kept smiling at Singleton. "I'll show you." He leaned, smoothed the dust and began anew to finger-sketch a diagram. "Here; this is the centre of the big plateau. You sit your horse here, pick out the highest peak—which is always shiny with snow—and never let it go to your right or left. You ride into the foothills and look for stone funnels of red rock. Go between them. Find the trail there and enter the mountains." This time as the buck straightened up, he was wearing a softly sardonic expression. "There were men a long time ago who came into the Taras from New Mexico and trapped and hunted. They have been gone many years. They did not find the secret Arapahoe camps. Last year there were hunters and cowmen up in the Taras too, but they did not really want to explore so they did not go deep beyond the foothills. Singleton, what I have just shown you is how to find the Arapahoe land back up in there."

Singleton was pleased at the trust. "I'll keep the secret," he said.

"No; I told you because I want you to come up and make a summer camp with us. I know where there are fish this big."

Singleton lightly scratched the tip of his nose while studying the width between the buck's hands. "Pretty big," he murmured in gentle doubt, and the Arapahoe laughed because he appreciated tact.

"I know where there are elk up in there, and bear, and sage-hens. Singleton, we will go up there soon now. You told me you were going over to Silverton. I showed you how to find the Arapahoe country because I want you to come soon."

These were reasons why Singleton had never drifted much north of Raton Pass. The main reason was because he did not like cold weather and was unaccustomed to it, being a South Desert rangeman. Another

reason was because from what he had
heard, range-riding in the high country was very different from the South
Desert, and Singleton had figured
that a man in his middle-thirties
might be too old to learn new ways—
especially when he did not have to
learn them; there was always plenty
of work for a tophand down south.

But this was a good friendship. It
was in fact a rare one between a
rangeman with blue eyes and a moun-
tain Indian whose strong tribal
affiliations were in evidence every
day.

Singleton had held forth a hand
and the buck had gripped it. The
following day the Arapahoes had
begun striking camp to go—
straggling Indian like—back up
towards their own highland territory.
Singleton lingered an extra few days,
then he had left too, heading for
Silverton, where he had remained
only a week before having his horse

freshly shod all around, buying an extra set of shoes, with the nails, which he stowed in his saddlebags, stocking up on salt and bullets, and striking out.

It was an adventure. It was also slow-going but Singleton was in no hurry. He seldom in his life had been in much of a hurry.

The land changed, not subtly the way it did on the desert, but abruptly and sometimes quite awesomely, as when he first awakened with the fog lifting and sat up staring at the Taras, the highest peaks he had ever seen in his life.

And the game, the timber, the water, the strong grass and the endless browse. It was to a South Desert rangeman, an almost totally different world.

He entered the foothills with the highest, glazed peak dead ahead, and located those red-rock spires with almost unsettling ease. He had simply memorised the buck's instructions. He had never attempted to commit them to paper.

From the red-rock funnels he set a fresh course towards the rougher, gloomier timbered country, and told his bay horse he thought they must be pretty close to the end of their trail.

They were, but it was not the end Singleton expected at all.

2

THE RENDEZVOUS

At the entrance to the shadow world of giant trees, a spongy carpet of ions-old layers of pine needles was noticeably indented where the trail went from the tough grass of the rolling foothills into the silence and gloom of a primaeval uplands.

It was not hard to imagine why strangers had never felt much desire to explore all this vastness with its darkness at noon, its other-worldly hush, and its feeling of total difference. To men accustomed to the wide sweep of open country, there had to be a very inhibiting effect once they were surrounded by silence and a closeness one never encountered upon the plains or plateaux.

Singleton was accustomed to open country too, but perhaps because he felt that he was welcome up in here the other feelings which ordinarily arrived simultaneously with abandoning the sunshine and the openness, did not bother him.

Also, he was concentrating upon the trail. He had not been very certain from back down by the redstone spires that he would be able to find the correct trail, or, having found it, that he would know which diversions to pursue if he encountered them.

He had no desire to have come this far, only to spend weeks lost in a jumbled world of alien things.

But he did not get lost. The trail was well indented, his horse followed it without difficulty, and while he did in fact encounter several forks, one rule of thumb kept him from taking any of them. There were no horse-tracks on any of them, but there *were* horse-tracks, old but discernible, upon the main trail.

Once, he thought he smelled smoke, but the wind shifted and the fragrance was lost. Another time his horse changed leads abruptly, and threw up its head, little ears pointing.

There had been a bear through this territory the day or night before; he had left his claw-marks on several trees and had demolished a blue-berry thicket, but he was no longer around, evidently, a fact which Singleton's horse required a lot of convincing about.

They crossed a cold-water creek. Both man and beast tanked up. They crossed a wide glade with rank rip-gut as high as a horseman's stirrup. There was a big bull-elk out there and his cow, heavy with calf. Neither of them offered to flee and in fact the roman-nosed bull stamped against the ground with his forefoot, hard, to make his warning.

Singleton estimated his size the same way he had been estimating weight in cattle and horses all his life, and guessed the bull weighed close to a thousand pounds, roughly what Singleton's saddlehorse weighed. Singleton reined wide around and left the big animals in their soggy glade.

The Taras were vast. Hundreds of miles deep and hundreds of miles east and west on a concave curve which seemed to create a huge, thick spine up the middle of a high-country's prostrate great form, all of it—or at least most of it—uninhabited, and with very few indications that even Indians had camped or lived there.

For Singleton, the South Desert man, it was like appearing in a fresh new world where few had gone before and where right at this time there were no other people around.

Game appeared often. So often in

fact that his horse became accustomed to the fact that the deeper they penetrated the more wildlife they were going to meet, and eventually the horse, while always alert and quick to discern movement, became just about as philosophical about the various varieties of game as his rider also became.

The day progressed but except for increasing heat down through the roofed-over forested area, and brilliant showings of golden sunlight across the parks and meadows, it would have been impossible to be certain; the gigantic forest monarchs were as ageless as they were timeless, and all those interlocking bristly treetops several hundred feet above, prevented changing sunlight to filter through so that Singleton would have been able to guess the time of day.

But he had a fairly accurate built-in physical clock; it hadn't failed him over the years and it did not fail him now. By mid-afternoon he guessed that he might have to make a camp and resume his search in the morning, but that was at best a guess. He had no idea how far up through here the Arapahoe would have gone. So far, it did not seem that he would have had to even go this far; Singleton had seen no signs of trespassers.

Later, though, when he was certain the unseen sun would be reddening on its slow descent into the west, he came across a wide trail coming in from the east, and here he found fresh horse-sign. Fresher in fact than the sign of barefoot horses he had been following since early morning, and this time the marks were of shod horses.

He guessed cowmen were looking for strays. He also guessed that if strays ever reached some of the lush, watered meadows he'd crossed, they would not voluntarily go back down out of here.

He picked up that fragrant smoke-scent again, a little stronger this time, and surmised that its source was not very far ahead because when he sniffed it now, it was not being borne to him by the wind. This time, there was not a breath of stirring air.

He was now following the shod-horse imprints which were freshly superimposed over the barefoot-horse marks. He told his horse that this huge, primitive country through which they had been passing all day feeling isolated and entirely alone, was beginning to look as though it were occasionally traversed after all, and in recalling the Arapahoe's sentiments about hiding his budding young daughter from alien influences, he recalled his own doubts about the buck's ability to do that, which now seemed about to be borne out.

The light was failing, finally, when he thought the smoke-smell was getting stronger. That was while he was climbing the trail on the lower side of a ledge which ultimately flattened so that when Singleton arrived upon its top-out, he could actually see the distant sun, as well as a hidden big long valley down below, surrounded on three sides of forest, and upon the fourth, southerly, side, by the flaky rock escarpment upon which Singleton was sitting.

Daylight would be gone in another couple of hours. He had a smoke up there while allowing his horse to rest, and later groped for the downhill trail through all that tallis-rock to the long valley. Here, he finally saw an occasional wisp of grey smoke rising. He smiled; that was exactly the way he and the Indians had 'made meat' miles southward. He had a premonition that he was closing in on his former companions, and he knew exactly what he would find, a typical Indian encampment, cluttered and dusty and picturesque.

Then he crossed the long valley following smoke-puffs, looking alternately for tracks in the thick, coarse upland grass, and also looking for hobbled Arapahoe horses grazing somewhere within sight.

There were no horses, but the smoke, which drifted in tendrils, remained, so he finally concentrated upon that alone, and pushed through the meadow to a spit of firs and pines near the yonder base of the rising granite, and saw through a fringe of second-growth where a second, much smaller little glen was. He could see what appeared to be lodgepoles out there, and when he got closer he could in fact actually see the lodge, but not too well yet as he cut back and forth through the trees to reach that little glade.

Then he broke out of the trees into the glade—and his breath stopped for several seconds. The smoke was rising over a place of devastation. The lodge had not burned, although its hide walls still simmered where someone had tried to torch it, but merciless hands had dragged all the parfleches and panniers over, had emptied out their contents, had kicked and tossed personal belongings in all directions, then had fired the litter.

There was no sign of livestock. The lodge flap had been torn half away and now hung forlornly as Singleton reached down to tug loose the tie-down thong on his sixgun before slowly dismounting and standing back for a moment or two making certain whoever had done all this was not still around.

He tied his horse in the trees out of sight and went ahead on foot.

The squaw was dead inside the smouldering tipi, shot at very close range. The buck was north of the lodge with a Winchester rifle behind him. The wooden stock had been smashed by a bullet. The buck had been hit several times, and brightly shining in the grass were three brass casings. The buck had managed to fight at least very briefly before dying with two bullets through his chest, one in his head, and another one through his throat.

Singleton turned slowly. Whoever had been here to kill these people had been very wantonly thorough. Nothing of value remained, and the things which had not been considered of value had been mounded roughly to burn. This was the smoke Singleton had been sniffing off and on all day.

He went out and around the perimeter of the little meadow, dreading what he expected to find. He put off going westerly, behind the hide lodge, until the very last.

She was back there lying on her stomach, shot from behind and mercifully dead almost before she rolled flat out in the grass.

A thick boot-sole had come down

across the child's personal treasure, grinding glass and frame into the ground.

It was the little mirror Singleton had given her down at the aspen-camp.

The sun steadily sank, balancing momentarily upon a high peak sending forth brilliant red rays which came filtering through tree-limbs like cathedral-light.

Singleton went back to hobble and off-saddle his horse. He moved deliberately and quietly. Later, he used his hat at the creek to douse the smouldering fire, and when that had been done, with no stomach for supper, he went to work making three graves, no simple feat since he did not have a digging implement.

In the end, with the cold night coming, he half-buried and half-covered all three of them, bringing huge-rocks to their last campsite to make three cairns wolves would be unable to desecrate.

He was dirty and sweaty and exhausted by the time it was all cared for. He washed at the creek, took his bedroll deeper through the trees, took both Winchester and Colt with him back in there, and bedded down. He was certain the men who had done that to the Arapahoes were long gone, still a man, unlike a cat, only had one life to gamble with.

He slept in a grey haze of weariness and grief. During the course of all he had done this afternoon and evening he had pieced together the sequence of events arising out of the fact that those shod-horse marks he had been following the last two or three hours had belonged to scavenging killers.

Those men—he thought there had been four of them, judging from the tracks—had somehow or other either known the Indians were up here in camp, or else they had seen them straggling up here and had let them pass, and had then started stalking them, but however the initial sighting had occurred, those men on their shod-horses had come through the trees to the little glade exactly as Singleton had done, had dismounted back in there unseen by the Indians and evidently remained completely hidden until the buck was returning from a hunt into the northward rocky territory, then they had drawn beads on him and had inaugurated their attack.

The buck had died fighting, but without a ghost of a chance right from the start because he had not only been unsuspecting, but he had been striding across the open glade towards his lodge without even any underbrush to drop behind when the firing commenced from the secreted killers in the forest.

After they had killed the buck, they came forth and caught the squaw inside the lodge. One shot had blown half her head away.

Lupin may have been killed even before that. Otherwise she would not have been back there behind the lodge with her mirror, sitting in the grass, she would have been fleeing.

They probably killed the girl at the same time they opened up on her father. In which case the woman would have been the last one to die.

Not that it mattered, exactly.

The horses were gone, five head of them. Three saddle-animals and two pack-animals. Good livestock, too. Singleton remembered admiring them.

Also, only one weapon was still in the burnt-out place of death; the rifle with the shattered stock. Otherwise, the pistol and carbine, like the horse-equipment and much else, had been taken away by the killers, who had also driven off the horses.

3

BAD WHISKY AND TALK

Singleton left in the dawnlight. There was nothing else to do. The hide lodge might stand all summer, and maybe even throughout the windy autumn, but winter snows would level it.

Those personal things, buckskin clothing, otter-hide tubes for holding hair-braids correctly, cooking utensils, skin-frames and blankets—were all left back there.

Singleton rode all the following day until he was able to halt near late afternoon high upon the rounding slope overlooking a stage-road to the east, the direction from which those scavengers had arrived, and the direction they had traversed with their stolen horses, afterwards.

He did not see them. He had not expected to see them, nor even their dust because they had departed from the devastated Indian camp hours before Singleton had even got up to the long meadow.

He began angling down towards that coach-road, finally, aware that as soon as dusk arrived he would be unable to follow the shod-horse tracks further, but satisfied about one thing: That tin-roofed town he had spied the previous morning very early, lying to the south-east, would still be down there, and with any luck those murdering scavengers would either have passed through that town on their way into the mountains, or would pass through it driving five stolen horses, on their way out of the countryside.

He left the trail completely, made

his own downslope trail, reached the
stage-road just at dusk, and turned
southward, finally on level ground
where he could boost his horse over
into a lope.

He saw the crooked sign before he
reached the town. It said, 'Cutbank 5
miles' and by the time Singleton got
down there to the outskirts, with
night closing in on all sides and with
Cutbank's lamps and lanterns beginning to brighten the darkness, he was
of the personal opinion that the
actual distance between that sign and
the town was more nearly seven
miles.

The liverybarn was upon the north
end of town, and it was also somewhat
isolated because aside from its own
network of pole corrals, south of the
barn was the working-yard and depot
of the stage company's Cutbank
installation, which, also having big
corrals and a large fenced-in yard
further isolated the liverybarn.

All this amounted to a convenience, because in most towns there were people who vociferously disliked having unfragrant and fly-drawing liverybarns within town limits.

As Singleton turned into the wide yard out front and a liverybarn night-man came forth smiling and smoking, to take the reins when Singleton dismounted, a large cinnamon-coloured hound-dog ambled forth, bony big tail wagging, to also add his welcoming broad smile. Under different circumstances Singleton would have been impressed. Not many cow-country towns were this genial to newcomers.

Singleton left instructions as to how he wanted the horse cared for, paid in advance, then strolled to the plankwalk out yonder, and as he reset his hat and studied Cutbank it occurred to him that while just about everything else in this highland country was different from its counterparts where Singleton had come from, the town was not very different at all.

He went across, bypassed the saloon for the cafe, and ate his first stove-cooked meal in several months in a place where he sat at a counter, practically alone at this time of night, drank coffee, ate pie and stew, drank more coffee, and smilingly discussed the weather, the mountains south of Cutbank a good many miles, and even national politics with his host, the pot-bellied big cafeman who had at one time been an awesomely powerful individual, but who had for some years now been running to seed, and showed clear indications of it.

In response to Singleton's casual mention of redskins the cafeman's mouth pulled down. "Naw; not around here," he pronounced. "At one time, sure, we had 'em just like everyone else had 'em, but there ain't been none around here in a long time. Oh; once in a while someone'll swear

up and down they seen In'ians back
in the mountains. That usually hap-
pens about huntin' season, you understand, when it's cold and fellers pack
a quart of old blind-staggers up into
the hill with 'em. But hell, there's no
In'ians been around here in years."

Singleton sipped the remainder of
his coffee before saying, "How about
horsetraders? You surely got them in
Cutbank."

"Yes indeed," agreed the cafeman,
padding over to fill himself a cup of
coffee. "Yeah; there's Milo at the
liverybarn. Milo Harrington. He
owns the place. He does a lot of
trading. In fact, when I first come
into this country old Milo had oxen.
The best pullin' animals around, for a
fact. Well; old Milo'd trade for
anything ... Then there's Bruce Hen-
derson. He trades a lot. In fact I'd
expect a man would be safe to say
Bruce just about has taken it all away
from Milo. Only I figure Milo is

probably tickled pink, 'cause running a liverybarn takes just about all the time a man's got."

Singleton said, "Where does Bruce hang out?"

The big cafeman made a casual and all-inclusive gesture. "South end of town. There is a stone wall out front of his house. You can't miss it."

Singleton finished the coffee, put down some silver, smiled at the paunchy cafeman and walked back out into the night, turning southward.

He estimated that he could spend about as much time in Cutbank as it might require for him to get some kind of a lead on the horse-stealing killers, bearing in mind while he was talking to people that those murderers would be steadily widening the distance between themselves and Singleton.

Delay or not, he had to pick up some idea of the direction he should ride in; He had to also determine whether or not anyone in Cutbank might be able to offer that information.

He had a hunch that the killers would want to peddle those Arapahoe horses quickly, and not just because they would want some cash money but also because driving loose-stock when someone was on the run, was a little like dragging a lead weight. Experienced raiders were fully aware that the surest way to avoid apprehension was to move fast, and keep moving fast.

But the horsetrader knew nothing. He stood on the porch sucking his teeth, listening to Singleton, and shaking his head. "I never saw any horses like those, mister, lately, and no one's come by offering to sell me five head in about a month. I sure wish I could help you, but ..." The trader hunched thick shoulders.

Singleton turned back up towards the centre of town where the saloon was. Upon entering Cutbank he had felt almost totally confident. Now, he was beginning to think he had misguessed, that the killers had not turned southward from the mountains but had probably headed on easterly, or maybe even northward up the coach-road.

He paused in front of a harness works to slowly roll and light a smoke, then to stand upon the lip of the plankwalk considering the high, star-bright sky, and wonder whether he had not been foolishly assured, when in fact with each passing moment from now on his chances of ever really finding those killers lessened.

A tall man who had been leaning in layers of shadow along the front wall of the adjoining storefront had noticed Singelton, had watched him roll the cigarette and to afterwards stand solemnly upon the edge of the sidewalk. The tall man shoved upright and walked forward to say, " 'Evening, friend. I'm Ed Bradley, Town Constable. Sure is a pretty night isn't it?"

Singleton turned. The constable was about four inches taller, but not as compactly thick nor solid. "Fine night," Singleton agreed.

"Find those horses you was looking for?" asked Ed Bradley, idly gazing northward across the roadway where several rangeman were walking their horses down into town.

Singleton studied the lawman's lantern-jawed, weathered profile. That damned cafeman evidently had a tongue which hinged in the middle and flapped at both ends. "No," he answered. "I went and talked to the horsetrader south of town. He hasn't seen them either."

Bradley turned back. "Someone steal them from you?" Singleton considered his answer carefully, unsure whether taking this cow-town constable into his confidence would help or hinder. He evaded an explanatory answer by saying, "No, they weren't stolen from me. They belonged to a friend though, and I just came from his camp, and the horses were gone."

Constable Bradley considered this. "Was your friend at his camp?"

"Yeah, he was there all right," replied Singleton dryly.

"Well; didn't you ask him where his horses was?"

Singleton guessed it was inevitable that if he remained in conversation with this lanky individual long enough, he'd find himself being badgered into a corner. Now—he was indeed cornered. Short of rudely walking away without replying, or lying which had even less appeal, he was going to have to tell his story.

The tall man was gazing at him, awaiting an answer. Singleton lamely said, "They were In'ian horses," and the lawman kept looking at him as though he expected more. When that was all Singleton volunteered the constable spoke sardonically.

"Lots of folks got In'ian horses. Mind telling me you name?"

"Singleton. Grant Singleton."

"Mister Singleton, you sort of interest me. Getting you to talk about these horses you're looking for is like pulling teeth, so I figure there's a story behind it." Bradley rarely smiled but right now he came close when he said, "Tell you what, unless you're religious soul and got something against it, I'll stand the first round at the saloon. And we can talk about those horses. How many did you say there was?"

Singleton did not recall mentioning the number. "Five; three ridin' horses and two pack animals."

Ed Bradley accepted this with a little nod. "You care for that drink?"

Singleton did not care either way. He was not in the least averse to drinking, nor was he enthusiastic about it. What tipped his personal scales in favour, was the fact that he had not had a drink since leaving the south country, down around Silverton, and that had been almost a month back.

They hiked up there side by side, and when they entered a faded, bronzed and wiry-looking rangerider turned and called over. "Hey, Ed, I looked for you a while back at the jailhouse and couldn't find you. The old man said for me to hunt you up in town tonight and tell you some son of a bitch run off six or eight of our using horses which was runnin' loose towards the foothills."

Singleton stared. "When?" he asked, and the wiry cowboy looked a little sceptically at Singleton before replying. "Last night; maybe late yesterday afternoon or evening; wasn't no one up there until this morning, and the sign was pretty darned fresh."

Constable Bradley said, "I'll look into it, Seth. You tell Mister Hudspeth I'll make a ride out and around."

The rangerider seemed not entirely satisfied, as he faced forward to reach for his refilled whisky glass. "You put if off for very long," he mumbled, "and there won't be much point in even going out to look around."

Bradley acted as though he had suddenly developed deafness, and led Singleton down where the bar made a smooth but abrupt curve towards the wall. Down there, there were no other drinkers.

When the barman arrived, brows raised, Bradley said, "A bottle, Lefty, and two glasses." Then he turned towards Singleton. "Your friend's camp—it was near the foothills?"

"Beyond them a goodly distance into the mountains."

"All right, I missed on that one. But his camp was north-west of here."

Singleton nodded and watched the barman set up their bottle and glasses.

"Mister," said Constable Bradley, "that's where the range of this cowman named Hudspeth lies. My point is that someone over there has been busy stealin' horses ... Mister Singleton, say when."

"When!"

Bradley tilted back the bottle, considered the contents of Singleton's glass and said, "You're not much of a drinking man. Well; to tell you the truth neither am I."

He filled the second glass, stoppered the bottle and pushed it back, then without touching his glass hitched half around and said, "Outside on the sidewalk you was cagey as a sore-tailed bear, Mister Singleton. Now I'd admire it if you'd tell me straight out. Was those In'ian horses that belonged to your friend stolen?"

Singleton lifted his glass. "Yeah." He downed the pop-skill, felt water start in his eyes, and also said, "Stole the five damned horses, Mister Bradley, shot my friend four times and killed him. Shot his wife in the face and shot their little girl in the back of the head."

He raised a dirty cuff to squeeze away the water from his eyes. "That's the gawddamndest whisky I ever tasted in my life."

Bradley nodded understanding and still refrained from touching his whisky glass. "What was your friend's name?"

"Some damned thing," replied Singleton, "that I never could pronounce so I just called him Pete."

"In'ians?"

"Yeah. 'Rapahoes."

Constable Bradley continued to watch Singleton for a while before saying, "Walk on down to my office with me and we'll make a pot of coffee and talk."

"All I want to know," stated Singleton, "is which way they drove off with those In'ian horses, and I came down to Cutbank because I saw the tin roofs and figured they'd probably light out in this direction to have a drink or maybe buy supplies."

"It won't take long to talk, Mister Singleton."

The whisky bottle was a continuing offence to Singleton so he turned away from it, studied Bradley's expression briefly then said, "All right; lead off."

4

CLUES

When Singleton finished, the lawman snapped his fingers before saying, "I think by golly we just might be able to pick us up a little something at that." He arose and set aside the coffee cup he'd been nursing at his desk. "Come along."

They hiked the cooling night in a northward direction to the end of town and entered the liverybarn like men on a mission. But the nighthawk was no help, so without a word Ed Bradley led off across the roadway and eastward beyond the main roadway, back where a number of residences were situated, every one of them sporting a picket fence out front.

The liveryman was at supper when Constable Bradley knocked on his front door, so he came to open the panel and display a fine linen napkin which was tucked into his collar at the throat, and which flared majestically on both sides of his vest, where it had been tucked in again at the the armpits. Short of upsetting an entire soup-bowl, the liveryman's front was adequately protected.

He was greying, heavy-set man with quizzical eyes and a square, granite-like jaw. He nodded without smiling and eyed Singleton, whom he had never seen before, with doubting interest.

Constable Bradley was a tactful man. He did not look as though he might possess tact, but in fact he had quite a lot of it. "Milo," he said. "I'm right sorry about busting in on you at suppertime, and all, but I got a problem and I figured when it involves horses, you're the best man in town to go talk to."

The unsmiling liveryman loosened a little. "Any way I can help, Ed. Any way at all."

"Few days back there was some grubliners camped at the public corrals out back of your barn ..."

"Yeah," assented the liveryman, his mouth drooping. "Sort of like darned gypsies. I told my men to lock the harness-room when they wasn't in it, and to keep a close watch. I've seen men like that before. Scavengers, thieves, worthless drifters and saddle-tramps."

"Did you talk to 'em by any chance, Milo?"

"Yeah. I went out the first night after they set up, and tried to figure them out. They told me they did a little horse tradin' now and then, that in fact they'd just come back from a camp where there was some nice animals they might get hold of later on, and would I be interested. I said I'm always interested providin' folks can give me a legal bill-of-sale, and also providin' I don't have to pay too much, and if the horses is serviceably sound."

Singleton said, "How many horses did they mention?"

The liveryman glanced around. "Didn't say, mister. Just said horses." Milo peeled the napkin off his vest-front and wadded it as he studied the lawman's countenance. "What is it, Ed—thievery."

"At the very best," replied Bradley. "Otherwise horsestealin' and maybe murder."

The liveryman's lingering expression of annoyance over being routed from the suppertable faded to be replaced by a different look. He paused, then said, "I thought so. When I was talking to them I thought they'd turn out to be renegades; dirty, unshaven, shifty-faced, weasel-eyed men."

Singleton said, "Three or four?"

"Four, mister. They was having their horses fresh-shod when I was talkin' to them. I guessed from that they'd be leaving soon and it was damned good riddance ... When I was a young feller several of us teamed up to go hide-hunting. We had our camps raided twice. Both times we caught 'em, and I'm here to tell you except for the smell, those men who camped at the public corrals a few days back was the spitting image. Ed; who got murdered?"

Bradley replied tactfully. "I'm not right sure yet, Milo. Me and Mister Singleton here just got involved. But as soon as I know for a fact ..." He nodded at the liveryman. "I'm obliged to you. Apologise again for pullin' you away from the table."

Bradley led the withdrawal beyond

the picket fence. As they turned back in the direction of Cutbank's business area, Bradley walked slowly with both hands fisted into his trouser-pockets.

Singleton said, "Where does the blacksmith live?"

Bradley roused himself long enough to say, "That's where we're going now," then he lapsed back into his pensive silence.

The blacksmith, it turned out, was not at home. Later, with time to reflect, Singleton was not certain he would have remained at home after supper either, if he had been married to the blacksmith's wife—a big, busty, granite-jawed German woman with flaxen hair, pale eyes, and a foghorn-voice.

They located the blacksmith finally, upstairs over the poolroom where a man named O'Malley ran a card room. It was quiet up there, except for a little occasional desultory conversation in low tones, and it was foggy with strong tobacco smoke.

The blacksmith considered Constable Bradley's request that he step over to a wall-bench, with a look of mild annoyance, and mild curiosity. One of the players said, "Go ahead, Cyrus, we'll hold off until you get back. We need a spell to rest up anyway."

The blacksmith was not a tall man but he was as round and coarsely thick and oaken as a mash-barrel, and when he looked at Singleton there was a clear reflection of feistiness in his glance. He was not middle-aged yet, but he had that jet-black hair which usually seemed to turn silver around the temple early in life.

As he sat upon a wall-bench with Bradley and Singleton he said, "Now what have I done?"

Singleton said, "Shod some horses for some saddletramps a few days back, Cyrus. You recall the men or the horses?"

Without any hesitation the burly man said, "Yeah, of course I recollect. What of it?"

"How many horses?"

"Four, Ed. Get to the point."

"Can you remember those men mentioning which way they'd be riding—or anything at all that they said?"

The smith leaned back, frowned and considered his friends over at the card table. "Yeah; they was going to pick up some nice pack and saddle-back animals up-country a ways, and take them west to Firebaugh where there was a big demand for honest usin' livestock."

Singleton stared. "West ... ?"

The blacksmith turned. "That's what they talked about, stranger. Takin' 'em west." He put a scowl upon his face. "What's it about, Ed?"

"I'm not plumb certain, Cyrus, but maybe horsetheft and murder."

The horse shoer nodded very emphatically. "Sure as hell," he growled. "They'd be the kind. They looked like any kind of trouble you wanted to lay your tongue to ... By the way, one of them was a big 'breed and one of the others called him Tom. Maybe that was short for Tomahawk; you know how rangemen are with their names."

Singleton rolled a smoke and kept his counsel until he and Constable Bradley were hiking back down the outside stairs, then he said, "West my butt. When they left the In'ian camp they were driving those Arapahoe horses east, Constable, and I could read their sign as plain as day right over to the coach-road. Maybe they figured to go to some town west of here, then changed their mind, or maybe they just said that figuring the blacksmith was listening, but they didn't go west, at least not while I was tracking them."

Bradley did not talk. As he had done before, he walked along now, hands deep in trouser-pockets, lost in deep thought. He led Singelton down the roadway a short distance and across to the jailhouse. He lighted the ceiling lamp, hung it, then tossed aside his hat and went to a dusty cupboard and returned to the desk with a heavy wooden crate full of wanted dodgers. He gestured and said, "Pitch in, Mister Singleton. There's got to be a poster in this mess for a 'breed-In'ian named Tom."

Singleton had doubts. Men on the range gave each other names which changed from season to season and from range to range.

But he looked. He took half the pile and Bradley took the other half. It was Bradley who finally tossed a dog-eared poster with a picture on the face of it, to Singleton, then went over to the stove to stoke it and test the coffeepot atop the solitary top burner as he said, "That's five years back."

Singleton sat down to study the wanted flyer. The man whose swarthy, flat face was pictured on the dodger was named Tom Juniper. He was a half-breed Sioux from Upper Spirit Lake in Canada who had at one time ridden with the notorious Clancy gang of train-robbers. He was a killer, was considered unbalanced, and was wanted in Montana, Canada, Idaho and Wyoming. He had killed, robbed and raided. He was over six feet tall, stalwart in build, taciturn, and very dangerous when he was angry or drunk. The total in rewards added up to sixteen hundred dollars, which was impressive since neither Jesse James nor Billy Bonney ever achieved that eminence in reward money.

Singleton tossed the poster back

atop the littered desk and said, "All right. It doesn't say he's ever been in Colorado. It doesn't say much of anything except that he's wanted and folks that meet him should contact someone up in Montana."

Bradley turned with two cups of black java. "It also don't say he was involved with your 'Rapahoes, and it don't tell us where he's been the last five years. And hell—every third In'ian alive is either Tom or Bill."

"Then," stated Singleton, "he don't have to be the man with those killers at all."

Bradley smiled. "You wait. The blacksmith's got to look at the picture."

Singleton was perfectly willing to sit and sip coffee and reflect a little while Constable Bradley took the dodger and went forth into the night on his way across to the card-room.

When he returned he handed Singleton the poster. "That's him.

That's the 'breed Cyrus heard one of the other ones call Tom."

Bradley went to his unkempt desk, sat down and picked up the cup of tepid coffee, then he said, "Mister Singleton; if we had singing wires up here—telegraph—we could send off messages north, south, east and west, and darn well get ahead of 'em."

"But you don't have any singing wires," stated Singleton, rising to cross over and refill his cup. "What I got to know, Mister Bradley, is which way they went from the coach-road up where they reached it off the mountainside."

Ed Bradley leaned back and scratched under his hat, then reset the top piece with a loud sigh. "They was driving ten head of horses, Mister Singleton, so if it was daylight we could split off, you west and me east, pick up the sign of that big a remuda being driven along, and pretty well cinch it down because to my knowledge no one else has passed through hereabouts driving that many horses since midsummer last year."

Bradley swished his coffee, downed it dregs and all, then arose and pitched a brass keyring to Singleton. "To the cells beyond that oak door, Mister Singleton. All I ask is that you don't spit on the floor and in the morning you make up the bunk just like you found it. Me—I live at the roominghouse. I'll see you at sunup, when we can eat breakfast first, then go do us a little manhunting ... Good night, Mister Singleton."

"Good night, Mister Bradley."

5

PURSUIT

Singleton had a fair notion of the lie of the land down around Cutbank, and to the west, for although he had arrived in town after dusk the previous evening, all the former afternoon he had skirted around the thick bulge of northward mountainside at an elevation which enabled him to familiarise himself with all the lower grassland range-country south, east and west of town. So now he rode forth on a full stomach after a decent night's rest reasonably confident that he would be able to turn up the fresh marks of a driven bunch of loose-stock—if any such sign existed.

Also, he was confident Ed Bradley, over on the easterly range, would find the marks if they existed on that side of town.

Bradley seemed not only interested, he also seemed stubbornly dedicated to finding the killers—and the stolen horses. Singleton could not have asked for better co-operation than he had thus far received.

He smoked, felt the warming sunlight, rode due west on the premise that anyone passing around Cutbank to the west from the coach-road, and travelling from north to south, was bound to leave exactly the sign he was looking for, and in circumstances which were pleasant and favourable, he poked along eyes on the ground.

He encountered cattle two miles from town, and he saw some horsemen angling up-country into the deep shade of a bosque of oaks south of the foothills, but otherwise there were no tracks, at least not the kind.

he was watching for, although he eventually was three miles west of Cutbank.

He halted over there, strode over to the lip of a wide arroyo and stood gazing down into it—and there were the tracks!

About a third of all those marks had been made by barefoot horses. Two thirds had been made by shod-horses, and the most prominent tracks, because they were in the drag where no following horses rode over them, had been indented by horse which had very recently been shod. In fact the gnurling on the city-heads of the nails used on those freshlyshod horses still showed clearly, when Singleton slid down the crumbly bank of the arroyo and knelt for a closer inspection.

He climbed back up out of there, got astride and paralleled the deep arroyo for about two miles before it began to widen out, to become broader in width and narrower in depth.

Where he finally halted the arroyo debouched, and up there on the range again, those driven horses had also fanned out. They had not been driven very fast down out of sight in the arroyo, but up here in the plain again there was plenty of evidence that the raiders had put them to a mile-consuming lope and had kept them at it.

Singleton did not follow more than another mile before turning back and busting over into an easy gallop on his ride back to Cutbank.

He was unable to reach town despite his increased pace until mid-afternoon, and he might just as well have dawdled along because Constable Bradley was not in his office and in fact did not reappear in town from the eastern range until the sun was well on its way to its westerly rendezvous.

Singleton explained about the

arroyo, where it broke up and where the tracks led from there—straight south.

Bradley was hungry so they crossed to the cafe for an early supper, got seats down at the lower end of the counter where they could talk, and ordered two hearty meals.

Singleton's complaint was that he was losing time. He should have pursued those tracks instead of returning to town.

The constable ate and thought, and finally near the end of their meal, looked over and said, "I know the country south of here pretty well. To peddle horses wouldn't be too hard, but not until you got over about as far as Fletcherville." He kept gazing at Singleton. "We'd never overtake those fellers, the head start they got, if we tracked them. We'd have to quit each night and commence again each morning. But there's another way."

Singleton said, "What other way?"

"By stage. We can take the night coach, which'll be leaving Cutbank in another hour or so, and we can sleep—maybe—most of the way, and the coach'll set us down in Fletcherville by about four or five tomorrow morning. Mister, no one driving horses can make that good a time getting down there."

Singleton pondered, decided it was a good idea, and as he and the constable walked forth from the cafe, Singleton said, "I got a question, Constable. How far does the authority of that badge on your shirt reach?"

Bradley pointed. "That's the town limits. My authority goes just that far and not a darned step further." He dropped his arm. "But you know, Mister Singleton, all my life I've been against felons." He struck out across the road and when they reached the other side and stepped up, they were heading for the stage company's way-station.

Singleton stopped him outside the door and said, "You like In'ians?"

Bradley shrugged. "Not too well, no. But I like murderers and horsethieves a hell of a lot less. Mister Singleton, raiders who'll kill In'ians will also kill other folks. That's my point."

They went inside, bought two seats on the southbound evening coach, then went down to the jailhouse to wait, and while they were sitting in the constable's office a slightly stooped, lined and grizzled old cowman walked in to brusquely nod at Singleton, and to fix the constable with a bleak glare.

"You got my message about someone stealin' some horses off my foothill range," said the older man, "and there you set, like you got lead in your britches."

Bradley considered the older man in silence for a moment before saying. " Why don't you offer a reward

Mister Hudspeth?" and the old cowman yanked open the door and stamped out to slam the door after himself.

Singleton built a smoke, made
some adjustments in his mind con-
cerning his original opinion of the
lanky town constable, and when he
lighted up and blew smoke he asked
the question which was uppermost in
his mind, now.

"After we get down to Fletcherville, and if we find those bastards
down there, with or without the horses, what do you figure our chances
will be?"

"Depends on what we do," stated
the lawman. "The law around
Fletcherville is pretty strict. If we can
get the marshal down there to pitch
in with us, we'd best just throw down
on those men and disarm them, and
arrest them to be jugged. Maybe we
can fetch them back up here to be
held for trial." Bradley looked keenly

at Singleton. "What did you have in mind?"

Singleton evaded a direct answer. He had the same thing in mind now that he'd had in mind during that long, bad night when he'd buried the three Arapahoes, but mentioning it was not going to make Singleton looked very good. There were a lot of people who willingly leant on lynch ropes and who drew steady bead from cover and executed outlaws, but nothing was said, and to Singleton's way of thinking that was best, so now he simply smoked and studied his companion, and said, "Depends. If they want trouble I got in mind giving them all they can handle. If they don't want trouble I'm for seeing them sentenced by a judge."

Ed Bradley nodded. "Nothing wrong with that. Well, we'd best get back on up to the way-station."

When they left the jailhouse office in full darkness another high-country

night was descending, with its chill
and its velvety gloom.

They reached the coach, tied their
horses to the trail-gate, threw their
saddles and saddle-roll into the stage
and climbed in. They were the only
passengers.

Across the roadway a merchant
was locking his front door for the
night, and up in front of the saloon
which was also on that opposite side
of the road, four rangemen, faded
and weathered and lean from hard
work and long hours of saddleback
time, were idly conversing with
cigarettes drooping from their lips. It
was a little early for anyone to be
piling up bar-time yet.

The stage was in the corralyard out
back, but its hitch was on the tongue
and the gunguard, bundled in a
moth-eaten old buffalo coat, wearing
smoke-tanned gauntlets and with a
rifle, a shotgun and a holstered Colt
with a yellowing ivory sets of grips,

was ready to start up over the fore-
wheel.

The driver was in earnest conversation with the stationmaster. The
driver was a tall, thin, hawkish-
looking individual and the stationmaster was short and thick, bundled
to the throat in a heavy coat and
wearing a muffler.

They collected their horses from
the livery stable, but carried their
saddles and gear and set out for the
stage.

When they were ready to roll the
whip talked down his rested and fed
big horses to keep them from violating
a town ordinance about four-wheeled
vehicles moving out of a walk within
town limits. The horses were ready to
hurl themselves into their collars. The
fact that it was a chilly night con-
tributed a little, otherwise the stage
company kept only sound, big usable
horses, mostly under nine, which
meant that once they had been rested

and fed and allowed to get restless in stalls before being hitched onto the tongue, all it would take to start them down through town in a run would be for someone to pitch a firecracker under any one of them.

Singleton leaned out to look ahead as the horses cut wide so as not to notch wood with the wheel-hubs, then eased around and snake-like, finally, straightened up and lined out directly behind them as the entire hitch lined out southward, at a fast walk, with the whip on his high seat still having to talk down his horses.

Singleton pulled his head back in, saw Bradley watching, and said, "What the hell are you doing this for—and don't give me that crap about felons and all."

Ed Bradley eyed Singleton for a long while without saying a word. When they were just beyond town limits down past the horsetrader's stone wall and the whip eased up on the lines, set back and whistled, and the horses hit their collar-pads hard and fast, the coach lurched and lunged so violently Singleton forgot what he had asked and Bradley forgot to answer it.

They covered three miles at record speed before the horses had their run 'out' and had picked up their second wind. The driver hauled them down to a little jog and let them maintain that gait for the next few miles. He was an expert, experienced coach-driver. He knew exactly how to conserve the power of his horses, and he knew the exact time to ease them out to let off steam.

But like all drivers, his passengers were not his first, nor even his second, consideration. They were his third and last concern.

No one had to explain this to Singleton. He had bumped his head twice on the roof of the coach, and he had lost his cigarette. He looked dis-

gustedly at Ed Bradley and said,
"Yeah—we can sleep most of the
way!"

Bradley didn't hear.

6

THE NARROWING PURSUIT

By Cutbank standards Fletcherville was a metropolis. It not only had a telegraph office, it also had a railroad terminal on the east side, out behind town, and along the main thoroughfare there were at least a dozen genuine red-brick structures interspersed among the older log and slab buildings.

It did not possess one saloon, it had three of them. It did not possess one cafe, either, as was true up in Cutbank. It had two cafes, two restaurants, and at the hotel which was actually an outsized rooming-house, there was a huge dining-room catering to anyone in off the road, but mainly to stage passengers and visitors who put up over night, or longer.

Fletcherville was also a county seat, which meant it had a *bona-fide* elected sheriff. Up at Cutbank, which was simply a cowtown in an unincorporated territory there was no sheriff because there was no established county, and the law, which was usually adequate, consisted only of Ed Bradley whose authority did not, technically nor officially, extend beyond town limits, but since most of the people up there were ignorant of the finer aspects of civilised legalities and book-taught jurisprudence, they expected Ed to act in his lawful capacity anywhere and anytime, and they generally supported him even if he pronounced edicts ten miles outside his official community.

Fletcherville was in fact an attractive community with elms on both

sides of a wide roadway, and with
plankwalks as well as wooden awn-
ings the full length of Main Street.

They put up their horses in the
livery barn when they arrived, leaving
their saddles and gear with the liveryman, who promised to see to their
horses and to look carefully after
their belongings. Then they set out
for the Sheriff's office, which was
placed almost in the centre of the
pleasant main street.

The sheriff was a stalwart man of
indeterminate age named Houston
Flannery. He held himself erectly
and looked down upon the world from
a height of better than six feet. In
fact Ed Bradley, who was tall and
lanky, had to raise his eyes a little
just to meet Sheriff Flannery's caus-
tic stare.

Flannery had two deputies, neither
of which were at his office when the
men from Cutbank walked in. In
fact, as Houston Flannery had main-

tained right along, any time a county law officer had deputies, and still had to run down trouble himself, he was a faulty administrator. Flannery had proceeded to prove himself a good administrator, then, by seldom leaving town, and by only rarely actually making an investigation even in town.

He listened to Ed Bradley with an impassive set of aquiline features, flicked a glance at Singleton from time to time during Bradley's recitation, and in the end he said, "Well, gents, you are plumb welcome to look around. We got several livestock dealers, plus McCormick's livery-barn. If I was you I'd start at McCormick's place. Fletcherville don't have a reputation for bein' a good place for horsethieves or any other kind of criminals to visit, but that don't mean we don't get 'em now and then." Flannery picked a paper off his desk and flicked it until it crisply rattled, then he glanced from it to his travel-stained visitors. "You got your badge with you?" he asked of Bradley, who dug the thing from a pocket and displayed it. "That's fine," stated Houston Flannery. "You go right on out there and make your investigation, Constable, bearing in mind we don't tolerate gunfights within town limits, and bearing in mind that whatever you turn up has got to first be cleared through me." Flannery offered a thin and humourless small smile. "After all, gents, I am the elected law official of the country and folks sure as hell look to me for enforcement and good detection. Those terms suit you, do they?"

Ten minutes afterwards when Singleton was rolling a smoke in the roadway, Constable Bradley sighed and while looking up and down the storefronts, quietly stated an opinion.

"That son of a bitch don't have a callous on his hands, hasn't been out in the sun in months, and leaves a man feeling like he's bein' used to keep that man in office."

Singleton, who had previously arrived at basically this same judgement, lit up and removed the cigarette to say, "You hungry?"

They went to one of the cafes. It was late and the place was empty. Also, the cafeman was dozing in a chair when they walked in from the roadway, and as he opened both eyes he did not look exactly pleased.

They ate like team-horses. It had been a long ride down-country from Cutbank, with few stops and no stops at all where food for passengers was available. As for the rest Bradley had mentioned up in Cutbank, they had got none of that either.

But when Bradley said something about going up to the rooming-house to reserve a couple of rooms for the night, Singleton said, "Go ahead. I'm going to commence askin' around."

They went together to McCormick's barn. McCormick was not there, nor did they expect him to be, but his nighthawk was. He was a burly, greying man who chewed constantly and who had a local reputation for being one of the most amazingly accurate expectorators in the entire county. He also turned out to be a very observant individual because the moment Ed Bradley mentioned a drive of about ten or twelve head of loose-stock the nightman, while rhythmically chewing, puckered his eyes at the pair of strangers, turned politely aside to let fly with amber liquid, then to say, "Some fellers was over east of town along the creek when I come past this afternoon bringin' in our harness-horses from McCormick's pasture. Four of 'em, and they had maybe twelve, maybe fourteen head of loose-stock."

"What did they look like?" asked Singleton. "Was one of 'em a 'breed?"

The nightman chewed, studied Singleton a moment, then spat aside before answering curtly. "Mister; I'm fifty-six years old. I got that way, and stayed plumb healthy, by minding my own business. When I see folks campin' I might wave as I lope past, but unless they beckon me on in—mister I just keep right on goin' and don't even look back."

The nightman swung his attention back to Ed Bradley. "You boys missin' some livestock?"

Bradley simply said, "We're lookin' around," and left it up to the nightman to create his own interpretation out of that.

Later, as they were strolling in the direction of the nearest saloon, Singleton said, "Sure as hell that's them. We should mount and ride straightaway, before they get too far."

Bradley thought differently. "Mister Singleton, if it *is* them, I'd be a little shy of ridin' up into their camp in the night. They could commence firing from fifty yards off and we'd never even see them. I'd say—let's bed down after a nightcap, and light out of here just ahead of sunrise. We'll be able to see them, with any sort of luck at all, before they see us coming. Thing is, would you know those In'ian horses?"

Singleton was confident of that. As they pushed through a pair of spindle-doors to become engulfed in the rank and redolent atmosphere of the saloon's one big, barracks-like room, he assured Bradley he could identify those Arapahoe animals.

They each had one jolt of rye whisky, looked and listened, marvelled that on a week-night there could be so many rangeriders in the saloon, and departed a little later to head for the rooming-house.

For Singleton, whose funds were far from inexhaustible, sleeping on a straw-mattress up off the floor, and with genuine army blankets to cover up with, was a luxury he could have foregone. Outside there was a thousand miles of uncluttered grassland. There were also barn-lofts and other places where a man could rest adequately without charge. On the other hand, he did not want to admit he was low on silver, nor did he want Constable Bradley to think of him as a cheapskate, so he paid twenty-five cents for the room with the cot in it, for one night, which was out and out brigandage, and made the best of it by sleeping like a log until his inherent rangeman's clock awakened him at four in the morning, and across the hall he heard Bradley also stirring.

Indians tanked up on drinking water to make certain they would not over-sleep. Rangemen, who were initiated to cow-camp life early and never afterwards were allowed to sleep later than first-light, just automatically awakened that way for the rest of their lives. Even the ones who quit riding and moved into the towns. Sometimes it was a plain curse.

Singleton did not think so. In fact he did not question early awakenings at all, even though he yawned and scratched and got dressed in darkness, then went out back to locate the wash-house, and found Bradley already out there.

They grunted at each other. Neither of them had anything to say until they'd ploughed ahead into the cafe with its frosty windows and ordered coffee first, then food.

It required a half-hour for the coffee to achieve its salutary effect. Then they hiked through crisp dawn to the livery barn, got their horses out and saddled them, and led them out back to turn them a few times before stepping up across leather. They were not taking the risk of the horses bucking because they were being mounted and their backs were cold.

The horses were thoroughly rested and fed, and they were slightly skittish as they rode down main street, which was already beginning to be busy.

Neither horse bucked but the one Ed Bradley was straddling had to be held checked up and short until they were northward beyond Fletcherville, ready to turn eastward towards the brightening, cold world where sunshine was not quite ready to pierce the grey, vague mists yet.

They had not asked where those men had been camping. They knew that the creek ran north and south. Bradley knew that, at any rate, and the champion expectorator had said the camp was along the creek, so they had to first locate the watercourse.

It was not a problem. In fact they saw mist, like a diaphanous great snake, rising over creek-water which was warmer than the surrounding atmosphere, an hour before they were close enough to discern creek-willows and berrythickets, and finally the watercourse itself.

The sun was coming. Over along the easterly rims a magnificent cloak of brightening pure gold light was above the sector of earth-crust where the sun was coming up.

Visibility was better than it had been up to this moment. Singleton studied the ground for horse-sign, found an endless display of it, mostly quite old, and gambled by pointing northward and striking out up in that direction.

His guess was based on that fact that the outlaws would probably have stopped when they were within sight of Fletcherville, coming down-country from up north. Ed did not dispute this; in fact he did not comment upon it at all, he simply reined his livery animal around and went hunched over and cold, following like an obedient hound-dog.

The scent of a cooking fire came down to Singleton, in among the creek-willows where Singleton was making his way with exasperation, because he was fearful of riding out in the open. He smiled over his shoulder. Bradley nodded but did not smile back. He was colder than he should have been, for some reason, and cold more than anything else had a demoralising effect upon some rangemen.

Singleton turned careful. He swung off, tied his horse, and while waiting for Ed Bradley to do likewise he stepped clear of the protective creek-bank cover and tried to peer north-ward.

Ed came up and said, "They're up yonder sure as hell." Then he qualified that. "Well; sure as hell *someone*'s up there."

Singleton returned to creek-side,

yanked loose the tie-down to his Colt, and led the way in a quiet, careful, sashaying walk in and out so that they were completely protected by sheltering undergrowth all the way.

Someone up there was frying meat. It had a delightfully tantalising fragrance, even to men who had eaten breakfast less than an hour and a half earlier.

Bradley found a deadfall and gingerly tight-roped across it to the creek's opposite side, and while Singleton waited, Ed made his cautious way through the yonder creek-willows and peeked out.

He stood a long while, then stepped onto the deadfall and by manipulating both arms as though he were a fledgling learning to fly, got back and said, "Horses by gawd! I couldn't see them all, but I could count six head up yonder about a half-mile, and there's smoke rising."

Singleton said, "From which side of the creek?"

Ed pointed. "The other side."

Singleton started towards the deadfall.

The smell of breakfast was clearer over along the opposite bank, and it was finally possible for the stalkers to see those horses, and to also see the rising white smoke.

Singleton was out front when they were close enough to hear a man clear his pipes with a fit of soggy coughing. They halted, waited a moment without speaking to one another, then as Singleton glanced back, Ed nodded his head.

"Another fifty yards," the constable whispered. "Singleton; chances are if they was in Cutbank they'll know me by sight."

For fifty yards Singleton stalked ahead as silent as a deer, then he halted where he could just barely make out men at a cooking fire, turned and said, "All right; I'll go up and palaver. But if there's trouble by gawd you'd better shoot first, and not hit me!"

7

SINGLETON'S PANTOMIME

The way Singleton accomplished contact was not especially astute, but it
seemed to work well enough. He
floundered through the creek-willows
which were especially dense up along
the northward reaches of the creek,
and when he got beyond them and
started striding towards the camp he
sang out and raised one gloved hand
in a high salute.

The surprised men at breakfast
looked up, did not move nor speak,
and sat like stone carvings until
Singleton was about forty or fifty
yards from them, then one of them
put down his tin cup very gently,

wiped greasy fingers down the outside seam of his faded trousers, and
quietly said something to the others.
There were not four of them, there
were five. But four of them were
unshorn, needed shaves, and were
brown with ingrained trail-dirt, while
the fifth man, although his shoulders
and hat were lightly dusted as though
from travel, was better dressed,
clean-shaven, and had linen which
still showed white even at the distance from which Singleton studied
the man.

The horses were almost as
interested in the striding stranger as
were the men at their breakfast ring.
Singleton glanced at the livestock
occasionally, as he got closer, they
left off looking at it at all when one of
the seated men heaved around and
stood up, thumbs hooked, sunken,
slaty eyes unsmiling and unblinking.

The standing man spoke with a

solid sound of suspicion in his voice. "Where is your horse?"

Singleton put off answering until he was closer, until he was among the creek-willows of their littered camp, then he jerked a thumb rearward. "Back a ways, tied in the trees." He looked at the seated men, met the unwavering black gaze of a big 'breed-Indian, considered the other men one at a time, then returned his attention to the tall, standing man.

"That coffee smells powerful fine," he said, almost smiling.

No one offered him a cup. The standing man said, "Why'd you leave your horse back yonder, and how's come you to come up here anyway?"

"I come up because I'm in the market for horses," stated Singleton, no longer attempting to ingratiate himself with smiling candour. "I left the horse back there because I never ride up onto folks before sunrise. Anything else?"

"Yeah," said a seated man. "One more thing. How'd you know we was up here with horses to sell?"

Singleton, who had already guessed that man in the black hat and coat who didn't belong with the others, was a horse-trader, answered bluntly. "A feller at the liverybarn over in Fletcherville told me there was horse-dealers out here camping along the creek ... Listen, gents, if you're not selling all you got to do is say so."

The tall man, still standing perfectly erect with thumbs hooked in his shellbelt, showed nothing, neither acceptance nor suspicion, but he studied Singleton carefully and after a while he loosened enough to say, "All right, mister. We got horses to sell. You want to walk out with me and look?"

Before Singleton could reply the man in the black coat struggled up off the ground, still holding his tin cup, and scowlingly protested. "Wait a minute, damn it," he exclaimed. "I been here an hour and a half ahead of this feller. By rights I get first choice. That's no more'n fair. I rode all the way out here and now you fellers are—"

"Oh for Chris'sake," exclaimed one of the men at the cooking fire, "let Shultz have first offer." This rangeman raised yeasty eyes to the tall man. "Sam; take Shultz out first. This other gent can drink a little coffee." The speaker turned and jerked his head at Singleton. "Get a cup, mister, and set right in amongst us … Shultz was here first. It's only fair he gets first offer." The unshaven, yeasty-eyed man suddenly grinned. "I heard there was a demand down here but I sure never knew it'd be this strong." He chuckled. "Or maybe we'd have brought fifty head instead of what's out there."

This man waved away the man named Shultz and the tall rangerider.

No one paid much more attention to Singleton until he had filled the place the trader in black had vacated, then filled the trader's two-thirds empty tin cup from their filthy and dented graniteware coffeepot. The 'breed Indian looked up.

"You from around Fletcherville?"

Singleton shook his head and tasted coffee before replying. "No. I travel through. I order-buy for some cow outfits down south, and now and then I take up a few head to speculate on." He met the raised glances of those three men with him at the breakfast fire.

The men ate and listened, and one of them, a long-faced sly-eyed man, said, "You got friends around Fletcherville, mister?"

Singleton nodded, giving look for look. "A few. I've been through here a lot over the past ten years."

It sounded absolutely believable but it was an out-and-out lie.

Singleton had not only never been in Fletcherville before, he had never been anywhere near this southerly sector of the north country in his life.

But the interrogator was not paying particular attention to Singleton's answer because his question had only been a sly prelude to what he said next.

"Can the sheriff in Fletcherville vouch for you?"

Singleton held his tin cup low and examined the long, narrow face of the outlaw, and slowly said, "Well now, friend, I trade in livestock for a living, I don't go running around buttering up county sheriffs. I don't even say howdy to them unless they say it to me first."

A youthful man, fishing fried bread from a greasy skillet, snickered. The man who had been slyly interrogating looked at the young man, then looked back at Singleton as though he thought he might not have caught it all, and offered an uncertain smile.

"All right, friend; come right down to it I never speak to 'em either, unless they talk at me first, and hell, sometimes even then I don't."

The youthful man snickered again.

Singleton had initially decided the tall man who had first challenged him was their leader, but since that seated man had given orders to the tall man, he was now prepared to make a fresh guess.

He addressed the yeasty-eyed man when he said, "I'd like to know ... Are those young horses? Are they serviceably sound? What kind of a price you got on them? Mister, if that feller dressed like an undertaker is a high-roller, then I'm wastin' my time because I just plain don't run a charitable outfit. I buy and sell for profit, pure and simple."

The yeasty-eyed man looked up slowly. He was older than the others, with the possible exception of the 'breed, but sometimes people of his background, colouring and formative environment aged faster than other people; at least *looked* older.

"They are sound animals," stated the yeasty-eyed man, holding out his cup for someone to refill it. "Two of them are broke to pack and follow along without being led. That's worth something, mister. The others are saddle horses without faults nor bad habits ... You'll see for yourself, they're quality animals ... Fifty dollars a head."

It was not an exorbitant price providing the horses were actually as sound and well-mannered and properly broke as the outlaw claimed, but in the cow-country it took one hell of a horse to bring more than thirty dollars, so Singleton cleared his throat, looked at the other men, who studiously avoided his glance as they ate and drank coffee, then waggled his head in what was either despair or resignation, and did not say a word.

The yeasty-eyed man warmed to his topic. "Let me tell you something, mister. This here is the pick of a *remuda*; there aren't no more horses like these within a hell of a lot of miles hereabouts. You're a travelling trader so you'd ought to know. We'll guarantee them to be without flaws nor vices and directly you'll be able to see that for yourself ... If we had the time and had the contacts like you traders got, we'd take them among the cow outfits or the town barns, and sell 'em off privately and one at a time for more'n we're offering them to you. But we can't do that. We're due west of here on a roundup next week."

Singleton heard the ring of conviction in the other man's voice and sardonically conceded that he had just been told the truth. Well, most of it had been the truth anyway, so he smiled and nodded his head, then turned to look out where the tall outlaw and the horse-trader in the black coat and hat were clearly haggling. The horses out there, bunched slightly together and maintaining a little distance between themselves and the other animals, were the Arapahoe stock.

"I figure you know what you're saying," he replied gently, and turned a smile upon the yeasty-eyed killer. "All right; we'll see what we can work out after I look at them. Providin' the gent in the black coat don't buy them first."

The answer to that was predictable. "Maybe Shultz will buy them, mister, but he won't get it done until after you've had a look and made a bid."

Singleton sipped the bitter black coffee, sat on his haunches and casually looked southward down through the creek-willows behind that outlaw with the menacing eyes.

He saw nothing back there. In fact, if he *had* seen anything, he would have sweated more than he was sweating.

This was the first time in his life he had ever done anything like this. In fact, it was the first time in his life that Singleton had deliberately set out to find someone and kill them. He had never been a lawman, nor any kind of a bounty hunter, he had been a rangerider and nothing more.

Nor did he have any illusions about the outcome of a shooting match if those four murderers got suspicious enough to throw down on him. And yet despite all this he felt a little exultant to be in their camp with them. He was satisfied they had no idea anyone from up in the Cutbank country could be down at Fletcherville looking for them yet, and as a matter of fact no one would have been down there, if Singleton and the Arapahoe buck hadn't agreed to rendezvous in the Taras about a month earlier.

Fate sat back and pulled strings, Singleton told himself as he drained the tin cup and tossed it aside, and people reacted like those marionettes he had seen Mexican players manipulate when carnivals came to the South Desert towns from deep in Old Mexico.

He looked off to his right. Shultz and the tall outlaw were slowly making their way back in the direction of the camp. The tall man was walking with his head down saying nothing but the horse-trader in black was pointing back at the loose-stock, was gesticulating and was speaking fervently like a man trying his utmost to make points in a dispute which he alone seemed willing to keep alive.

One of the men at the campfire also looked out there, and grunted. "That son of a bitch'd stutter if someone tied his arms behind his back."

8

THE TRADERS

The man with the menacing eyes arose soundlessly and walked out to meet the tall man and the horse-trader. He had clearly done this in order to get Shultz's highest offer without Singleton hearing it, and while Singleton guessed this was what was afoot, he was also beginning finally to worry about something else. Suppose Shultz did not make the highest offer; suppose Singleton made it and the outlaws accepted it—how was Singleton, who had exactly seventeen silver cartwheels to his name, going to pay for those horses?

The 'breed looked from beneath a

greasy, down-drooping hat brim and said, "Hank'll sweat them out." He did not say whether that meant the leader of the renegades would extract the last red cent for the stolen horses, or whether it meant something else. Singleton looked at the 'breed but there was no hint of meaning in his thick, murky features.

One of the men arose from the fire and went over among the unkempt litter of saddlery to rummage in saddle-pockets for a sack of tobacco with papers. He was rising up when he suddenly stopped moving and stood awkwardly bent and tense for a long time before he called to the others.

"Riders across the creek. Come over here; you can see them."

The sound of the man's voice even made Singleton start to his feet, but he remained at the fire as the others swiftly rushed across to look out through underbrush and willows to the far side of the watercourse.

It was a bad moment, but only briefly, then someone growled. "Gawddammit, Ace, you're worse'n an old granny for getting spooked."

They returned to the fire but the 'breed remained over near their equipment to watch what someone surmised was nothing more menacing than three cowboys riding diagonally from across the upper countryside from the north-east to the south-west, and evidently they had not seen the horses upon the far side of the creek, nor the breakfast smoke which had been dying down for more than an hour now, because they loped blissfully past a mile out and did not even look around.

Singleton turned to the youthful outlaw, the one who had snickered earlier, and asked the name of the band's leader. He got a sidelong grin with the reply. "Hank Foster. Why?"

Singleton grinned back. "Never hurts when you're tradin' to know a feller's name."

The younger man said, "Won't help you one darned bit this time, mister. Hank don't give a damn whether you call him by his name or not."

The 'breed returned to announce that those cowboys had not even looked to their left and were now heading arrow-straight for Fletcher-ville. Then he looked at Singleton to say, "I've seen you somewhere before," and Singleton shook his head without a qualm.

"I doubt it. Maybe, if you've ever traded down around the South Desert—maybe around Tucson or Tubac or maybe even up around Raton—but I sure don't recall you."

The 'breed lapsed into silence. Moments later Shultz walked to the camp, put a surly glance towards Singleton and jerked a thumb.

"Go on out there, Hank's waiting."

Shultz fished forth a cigar and rolled it between his palms as he looked at Singleton. He clearly wanted to say more, but was being inhibited by the other men close around. In the end, as he plugged the unlighted cigar between strong teeth, he said, "Some of 'em are footsore and you'd ought to look 'em over right close before making an offer."

An outlaw turned on Shultz. "Hey! what the hell do you think you're doing, with that kind of talk?"

Shultz sat down and lighted his cigar, ignoring the men around him, but intently watching as Singleton walked out and joining the outlaw-leader where Hank Foster was painstakingly rolling a smoke. When Singleton arrived close by, Hank Foster spoke to him withoout looking up.

"Mister Shultz is a tough trader. I hope you're not. Otherwise don't nobody buy our livestock today, and we'll maybe have to take them on down-country to the next town."

Singleton said, "There is McCormick in town. He's got the liverybarn. He buys and sells."

The outlaw lit his smoke and turned as though he had not heard. "Them three are the toughest of the lot. Two of them—that sorrel with the light mane and tail, and that steel-dust grey, they pack as well as ride. The other three just ride, but they well-broke and don't have a mean habit amongst them ... Let's get a little closer."

Singleton's heart hardened the closer he got. He knew those horses from another time and another kind of camp. The smallest one, chunky and sassy, had belonged to the little girl. She had told Singleton all about him one night at their cooking-fire, and he had gravely listened.

He wanted to know which of those

renegades had shot the little girl in the back of the head. He strolled the grassland behind Hank Foster, and halted when the Arapahoe horses began to edge nervously away. That was as close as anyone was going to get who did not have a rope on the animals.

The outlaw said, "Well; how do they look?"

Singleton answered stiffly. "Like forty dollars a head."

Foster snorted. "Hell; I got forty-five on 'em from Shultz."

It was probably a lie but one thing Singleton was sure of; those outlaws were not going to allow Shultz and Singleton to make any comparisons, so Singleton walked a little closer, then walked out and around, and returned to Foster's side as he said, "Fifty, then, and that's the absolute top dollar. Fifty each for those horses, now let's go look at the others."

Hank Foster looked pleased,

something Singleton noticed from the side of his eye.

The other animals were older and larger and wore discernible brands. They too, were good livestock, except that to a man as experienced as Singleton they were bred and broke for a different kind of use. These were someone's top stock-working horses.

Hank Foster plucked a long blade of wheat grass and chewed it as he said, "No colts, but prime cattle horses. They don't come any better. Let's walk." He led Singleton around this second bunch of animals. There was no way to dispute what the outlaw had just said, either, these were the kind of sound, sensible, bred-up using horses stockmen paid a high price for, to own, and the kind they would kill men like Hank Foster without going near the law, for stealing.

Singleton complained. "We're gettin' involved with a hell of a lot of money, Mister Foster—Hank. They're good stock but ..."

"Well, gawdammit," exclaimed Foster, "you come out here to buy horses didn't you?"

"Of course I did, but I wouldn't pack around that kind of cash for all the horses in Colorado."

Foster threw up his hands. "Hell; that's nothing. I wouldn't do it neither. But you got funds in Fletcherville?"

"Sure; in the safe at the general store," lied Singleton, feeling relief flooding through him as though he had just downed a big drink of whisky. "You fellers can ride on in with me this afternoon, help me corral the horses and I'll go over to the store and ..."

"Fifty dollars a head all around," demanded the outlaw.

Singleton stood glowering at the livestock and fidgeting with his feet. "I'll tell you for a fact, Hank, there's two out there I don't think will bring me ..."

"We told you the gospel truth," broke in the renegade. "The absolute gospel truth. There is not a bad habit amongst the lot of them, and they are every blessed one of them usably sound!"

"Well ..."

Foster slapped Singleton on the shoulder. "You can look anyone in the eye you peddle them to, and come back a year later and still look them in the eye. I'm not lyin' one bit to you."

Singleton moaned. "All right. Fifty dollars a head. You fellers help me drive them to the public corrals down at Fletcherville and I'll get you your money."

Foster shoved out a soiled hand. Singleton gripped it, released it and turned. "It's done. We done made our trade and shaken on it so there'll be no backin' out. Now tell me—what did Shultz offer?"

The man with the menacing look threw back his head and laughed aloud. he took Singleton's elbow and started back to camp and did not answer; in fact Singleton never did determine how much the horse-trader dressed like an undertaker had offered, but when they reached camp and Shultz read in Hank Foster's face that he had lost out to Singleton, a venomous expression showed briefly before the trader dropped his smoke into the coals of their recent fire and said, "Next time, you boys'll want to think about something. When a feller is established in business in a place, he can do you a lot more good than some fly-by-night trader who comes and goes."

Singleton thought it was a bad thing to say to men like those renegades who were thieves and killers, but perhaps Shultz did not know about that. Maybe he thought they were simply rangeriders with a little remuda they wished to sell, and which they had obtained legally. But it was hard to accept that. At least to Singleton it was hard. Those outlaws looked exactly like what they were.

Still, Hank Foster did not take offence. He shrugged and said, "Mister; when a man's got something to sell he's just interested in one thing—a top price."

That ended it. Shultz left a little later, escorted out to his horse by the youngest of the renegades, the one who snickered easily and who seemed to find humour in just about everything. Or maybe it only appeared that way; maybe the youngest renegade was one of those unbalanced people who smiled over the same things other men frowned about.

Foster waited until Shultz was beyond hearing then explained the deal he had made with Singleton to his companions and only one of them had a comment. That was the tall, lean, suspicious-eyed man called Sam, the one who had first challenged Singleton. He said, "Seems to me, Hank, a feller figurin' on maybe buyin' someone's horses would fetch along his money."

Singleton had his retort ready. "Mister, a man can get stopped and robbed in this country easier'n you can shake a stick. I've had it happen, and from then on I've made a practice of just plain not carrying it with me. Even if it costs me a deal now and then. I'd rather lose a few deals and have my money, than make a few and get robbed."

Sam considered all this before addressing Hank Foster again. He seemed loath to address Singleton directly. He had acted the same way towards Shultz. It seemed to be an odd quirk of Sam's to act as though no one existed except his cronies.

He said, "If we got to deliver them horses to the public corrals in town, the sooner the better." He looked steadily at Foster after making this remark, his glance holding vestiges of a significance he thought only the other horse-thieves would appreciate, but as a matter of fact Singleton picked it up instantly. Sam wanted to get rid of the stolen horses as soon as they could possibly do it.

Foster went to the coffee pot, rattled it, poured the dregs into one of their dented tin cups and hunkered sipping. He ignored them all for a while.

Singleton wondered whether he had ought to suggest riding on in ahead to get the money. He had in mind saying this way there would be no delay; when they brought in the horses he'd be right there to hand over the cash so they would not have to linger if they chose not to.

Then Foster scotched that by

finally arising as he flung away the residue of the coffee, and saying, "Good idea, Sam. Let's get rigged out and move 'em."

Singleton said, "Take your time. It'll be ten minutes or so before I get down to my horse and ride back up here." He nodded and turned to depart—holding his breath for fear that grinning younger outlaw would want to escort him as he had escorted Shultz.

Instead of that occurring, Hank Foster said, "We'll round 'em up and have 'em ready." Then he looked at Singleton and said, "You never said your name, mister."

"Singleton."

Foster turned away as his men began stirring. "Let's get Mister Singleton's livestock movin', gents," he said, and did not pay any more attention to Singleton, who hastened southward down along the creekbank in and out among the willows.

9

A TROUBLED CONSCIENCE

Ed Bradley did not arrive down there where they had left the horses until Singleton was loosening the shank of his saddle-animal and turning the beast so he could then snug up the cinch. He saw Ed moving in and out of filigreed shadows closer to the creek. He saw him across a saddle-seat.

Bradley was shaking his head as he walked on up and stared. "I never saw anyone play-act as well as you did, by gawd, Mister Singleton. I tell you if ever there was a feller missed his calling ..."

"Crap," exclaimed Singleton looking nervously around. "I got to ride in with them to town and corral the horses then I got to ..."

"I know," stated the lawman, breaking in quickly. "I heard just about everything that was said in the camp, and I figured out from the way you and that renegade-bastard was acting out yonder what happened on the horse-trade."

Singleton looked northward. "I got to ride back up there. Can you get down to Fletcherville and fire up that sheriff, and have things ready so's when we bring in the horses he can close in?"

Ed was agreeable. "I'll do it, don't worry. I'll shag-butt down there keepin' to the creek-cover until I'm close enough, then I'll bust out for town. Singleton? You'd better figure on some way not to be around the corrals with them, though. Sure as hell there'll be trouble and shooting."

Singleton had been considering

this on his walk southward to the horses. He did not have what he thought was a workable solution, but he had the best of all incentives for finding one, and soon—he probably would be shot by either irate renegades when they found themselves entrapped, or by possemen from the Fletcherville countryside who did not know Singleton from Adam's off ox.

"Hustle," he told the constable, and started to lead his horse out of the trees to mount it.

Bradley was agreeable but he still had not expressed himself fully on the way he had been impressed, so now he called after Singleton, "I just never would have figured you to be that good at play-acting."

Singleton almost did not respond, but just before leaving the last of the creek-willows he turned and scowled. "You'd have done just as good and maybe better, if you knew for a blessed fact that if they got even a little bit suspicious they'd shoot you like they'd shoot a rattlesnake. I wasn't play-acting, I was lyin' like a son of a bitch to keep alive!"

He turned his horse, swung over leather and cut away northward without glancing back. Under these circumstances praise irritated him.

While riding up where he could see thin dust rising, he speculated on the reaction of that sheriff in town to the fact that neither he nor Ed Bradley had gone first to Fletcherville's official lawman before riding out and bracing the horse-thieves and killers.

All they needed now was for the desk-rider down there in his fine jailhouse office to get his back up and decline to help.

Hank Foster was waiting south of the camp. The other outlaws were across the creek with the loose-stock, keeping it milling with obvious impatience. As Foster saw Singleton he sang out.

"Kick that damned horse out; let's get this drive moving!"

Singleton obeyed, followed the outlaw-leader down through the underbrush and willows to the creek, splashed across and emerged bent double with a forearm in front of his face to fend off whip-saw-like willow limbs. When they broke clear and were in the open Foster removed his greasy, ill-shaped old hat and wig-wagged with it. At once his riders swept aside on both sides to permit the loose-stock an open route, and the drive got under way.

There was a world of difference between driving loose horses and loose cattle; one species was born and bred to graze their way overland and the other variety, with only one stomach, was born and bred to run for it. That was how those horses went—in a swift southward rush which the herders on both sides and in the drag of them only remotely guided.

Until the horses were 'run down' they were not very amenable to direction, and as long as the herders had them aimed in roughly the correct direction at the outset they did not worry very much. They had been driving these same horses, hard, for several days now and knew their capacities and their characteristics.

Once, Foster loosely reined over near Singleton and cried out. "Look there; you see any string-halt or chest-founder or stove-up?"

Foster spurred away in a flinging run without giving Singleton a chance to respond. There was no need for him to act otherwise. Singleton had already observed how serviceable the livestock was, nor had he ever entertained a notion that it was not serviceable.

There was a difference between

'sound' horses and those which were called 'serviceably sound'. In Singleton's experience—nor was he alone in this—there was not a horse past five years of age which could be honestly called sound, but splints, a little proud-flesh in old healed wounds, heel-scar tissue and broken teeth, among other things which did not really impair the usability of a stock-horse but which kept him from being classified "sound" caused no lessening of a good using horse's capabilities.

In fact there were probably very few horses under the age of five which could not be faulted either for injuries or conformation. Only green-horns talked of 'sound' and blemish-free horses.

The animals Singleton was riding behind now were in good flesh, they were tough and hard and willing. That mattered; little flaws here and there did not matter unless of course, like sidebones or ringbones or leaky lungs, they would eventually create serious debilities, and Singleton, like the horse-thieves, had enough experience to recognise in the running horses up yonder that there were none of those more serious defects. He knew five of those animals, had been around them at the aspen-camp and knew they were usable and strong. As for the horses stolen from that old cowman named Hudspeth up around Cutbank, a man only had to look at Hudspeth and listen to him to know that he was too seasoned a stockman to feed flawed livestock.

When the stock began running down and the rustlers began easing off to allow the horses an opportunity to slacken off, Singleton saw Hank Foster beginning to ease back to ride stirrup with him, and Singleton hauled down to a walk, looped reins on the horn and fished for his makings to work up a smoke.

When Foster came over he pointed with his rein-free right hand. "Town roofs about a mile or two." He dropped the arm and looked over as Singleton lighted up and trickled smoke. "You figure to peddle them around here, do you?"

Singleton guessed the worry behind that question, and shook his head. "Naw; I'll take them on south. Maybe quite aways south." He glanced casually at Foster. "It wouldn't hurt I don't expect if a man was to trail these horses all the way over Raton Pass down into New Mexico— would it?"

The clear implication to that statement was that these just could be stolen horses and Singleton knew it, or at least thought it possible. But he had not *said* it, and that made all the difference in the world. No one liked to be called a horse-thief, but especially genuine horse-thieves.

For a while Foster drifted along,

eyes pinched down, wolfish profile
side-viewed to Singleton as he
watched his companions closing
gently on the remuda to head it
correctly, then he said, "Well, Mister
Singleton, you do with these horses
whatever you figure you got to do.
But I'll tell you something. It might
be a good idea to take them on down
the pass into New Mexico." He turned slowly, unsmiling and narrow-
eyed to exchange a look with
Singleton. It had been the same as
tacitly admitting the horses were
stolen.

Singleton picked words carefully
from this point on. "For fifty dollars,
Mister Foster, or maybe a bit less'n
fifty dollars, I could probably handle
a few more like these. In fact, if we
could work something out, and if you
didn't feel beholden to Mister
Shultz ..." He took a long, slow drag
off his cigarette, then just as slowly
exhaled.

Foster looked saturnine. "Mister Shultz don't mean crap to me. Him nor no other trader. Except maybe if me and the boys could work up something. Like us supplyin' and someone else peddlin'."

Singleton nodded. "I sort of had something like that in mind, Mister Foster. You supplyin' and me buying them right from you, and takin' them off a ways and getting rid of them."

Hank Foster reached inside his filthy shirt, low, and vigorously scratched. He looked again in the direction of Fletcherville's rooftops before saying, "How would a man find you, later on? Maybe three, four weeks from now, if he had couple dozen head to sell?"

Singleton considered his reply carefully before offering it. "I'll write down the address in Tucson and the one in Fort Collins, up here in Colorado. You get word to me at either place a week before you expect to make delivery, and I'll rendezvous where you want to hold 'em. Like you did here."

Whatever Foster might have said was abrogated by Sam, the tall thin outlaw, drifting back to ask if one of them hadn't ought to ride in first and make sure someone else, freighters maybe or more dealers, hadn't pre-empted the public corrals.

Singleton had his heart in his mouth when he forced a very casual comment about this. "I'll do it, unless one of you fellers would rather. If the public corrals are being used I'll see about getting some of those corrals McCormick the liveryman has."

Sam did not once look at Singleton as he and Foster listened. Even when Foster said, "Good idea, Mister Singleton. You know the liveryman and don't none of us know him." He smiled. "We'll see you down there."

Singleton raised an indifferent hand, then eased his horse over into a lope to go out and around the remuda. As he broke away Sam finally looked after him and said, "I never seen a dealer before who didn't have no money with him."

Foster snorted. "Go tell the 'breed to bend the drive to the far side of town, at the north end. That's where the liverybarn is."

Singleton studied the high sky for a clue about the time of day, then he turned his attention to the land on all sides, which was empty except for the distant coach-road, and over there a mighty and massive old freight outfit being ponderously pulled at a snail's pace by a ten-horse mule-hitch was grinding its way southward too, but it would be another two hours in reaching Fletcherville even though its driver and swamper would have the town in sight for that long, and much longer, before reaching the outskirts.

Singleton had been under strain for a long while. It had affected him in

several ways. Not only was he worried
and anxious, but he had the feeling of
being caught between two forces both
of which were hostile to him.

There was something else troubling
him. He had now been in the company of the men who had murdered
the Arapahoes for a number of hours
and instead of finding even one of
those men with a redeeming virtue,
he had seen each one of them as
someone he wanted to shoot to death,
and this was not something he had
ever felt before. He did not like it in
himself; it worried him. Not killing
Hank Foster. He could look forward
to doing that. Also the tall one named
Sam, who was clearly some kind of
dangerously upset individual—the
kind of a man who would shoot a
little girl in the back of the head.

But although he had entertained
some such deadly idea from the
inception of his manhunt, until very

recently he had not been face to face with the imminence of it.

He had never been fiercely vengeful, not even after burying the Arapahoes. He had been coldly calculating about finding the murderers and towards that goal he had done everything which he had thus far undertaken, and of course in the back of his mind was a conviction that there was going to be justice done if he ever found the renegades. ✗

Now he had found them; was in fact in more danger from them than they were in danger from him, and clearly a showdown was nearing, was imminent, and the tumult in his heart was very real, and yet he still disliked what his instincts as a rangeman told him he had to do.

When he came down near the environs of Fletcherville he untied the thong holding his holstered Colt in place, stood in the stirrups looking for Ed Bradley—or that stuffed-shirt of sheriff—saw neither of them and twisted to glance back. The horses were raising a fine dust about a mile back and they were coming swiftly.

10

UNDER FIRE ON THE WAY

Because events are generally shaped by the people in charge of them, it was entirely probable that Singleton should have expected difficulty. Ed Bradley could only do his best, and in a community where someone categorised as a town constable—the lowest law-enforcement denominator—from a place called 'Cutbank' would provoke smiles even in the saloons, and where a man of extreme ego officiated as senior law-officer, Singleton was more at the mercy of events than he expected to be, and yet he should have expected something like this to obtain because he had in fact met that county sheriff and had been adversely impressed by him.

In fact he had gauged the man so well that he had wondered about the sheriff's reaction to what Singleton and Bradley had done. The sheriff had warned them to see him before taking any action. They hadn't done it. It probably would not matter to that narrow and imperious county sheriff that they had been unable to do it, once they got involved with the renegades. He had left Singleton with the notion that he would not accept their excuses.

Now, as Singleton held his horse to a little jog and went ahead, across the stage-road in the direction of the liverybarn and the network of corrals at the north end of town, looking intently for whatever Bradley and the Fletcherville lawman had prepared by way of a trap, he neglected to look behind, and when he was close enough to see two idlers out in the tree-shaded yard of the liverybarn watching his approach, it was too late.

He was wondering about those two idlers. He was also looking for other signs of additional people down there, when he distinctly heard the horses coming and twisted slightly to look back.

It wasn't the loose-stock, it was a phalanx of hard-riding armed horse-men who had swept up across the stage-road from some cover to the west somewhere. They were extend-ing their line of advance until dozens of yards showed between the riders. They were hastening up behind Foster and his renegades, and at about the same time Singleton looked back, so did the outlaws, who no doubt until this moment had been unable to detect the pound of addi-tional hooves because their own hor-ses, both driven and ridden, made a closer and more resonant sound.

But someone's fluting high howl of alarm changed all that in an instant.

In a moment those wary outlaws who had been living out of their hats—and holsters—for so long, understood exactly what was happening. They did not, right at the initial discovery, have the time to reflect on *how* it had happened, but because they were habitually suspicious men, attuned to survival through deception, desperation, and violence, they would instinctively understand shortly now that they had been very deftly betrayed and trapped. They would understand, even as they exploded into defensive activity, that a *man* had to have set them up to be surrounded like this by armed and hard-riding possemen. They would have two suspects to reflect upon: Shultz and Singleton.

What was instantly clear to Singleton was the *physical* fact that those possemen were driving the renegades, with their loose-stock, directly down towards him, and there did not seem right at that moment to be anyone on ahead, except those two loafers in the shade of the liverybarn-yard to impede their progress.

It was far from an ideal situation. On the other hand, Singleton was out front with seemingly no interference, so he gigged his mount and ran like the wind to escape being in gun-range when the outlaws raced forward. There did in fact appear to be a very good chance he could reach the shelter of the liverybarn down the west-side backalley before the renegades could overtake him.

He rode with no illusions. Hank Foster would probably be suspicious by now. So would that strangely deranged tall outlaw called Sam, and the brutish-faced, muddy-eyed big 'breed Indian.

Men of that calibre did not require proof of anything; life meant little enough to them. They would shoot Singleton as they thundered past just because they might think it was possible he was the one who had led them down here into this trap. If Shultz the other horse-trader were riding along, they would just as callously shoot him. It was never a matter of proof with renegades, it was simply a matter of suspicion, and an opportunity.

He was so engrossed with looking back, where the loose-stock had by now detected the panic among the riders herding them along and were beginning to react with a head-up, high-tailed blind charge towards the Fletcherville main thoroughfare, that when the first gunshot sounded he was caught unawares because it did not come from far back where those belly-down racing possemen were striving mightily to close the gap, it had come from in front.

Singleton whipped around at the

precise moment the horse beneath
him bunched mighty muscles for his
next onward lunge, and high in mid-
air, suddenly folded all four legs,
dropped his head, and with Singleton
reacting in astonishment—too late—
the horse came down on his folded
legs, his belly and head, slid several
feet, then his rear-end kept rising
until he made a complete somer-
sault, momentum making almost an
inert projectile of his carcass. He had
been hit with a bullet squarely
between the eyes. He'd had no time
at all to be prepared for death; one
minute it was *not* there, the next
second it *was* there.

Singleton reacted with cat-like
instinct, the way bronc-riders and
horse-breakers schooled themselves to
react, but even so it was different
having a horse turn inside out
deliberately, and having one drop
dead instantly, so although Singleton
kicked loose of both stirrups and

leaned to catch himself standing up as the horse fell, when the catapulting body rose up behind, the saddle-cantle struck Singleton in the back over the kidneys, punching him violently forward and sidewards.

His sixgun flew from its holster, his hat sailed away like a wounded bird, and his body arched overhand then came down in a twisting jolt. He hit ground and slid. Somewhere ahead of him two armed men were firing carbines. He did not realise it, but they were both firing at him as he flopped and drunkenly skidded and rolled.

Behind him the loose-stock was veering away, towards the main road-way down through town. Otherwise they probably would have run right over the top of him.

People who had rushed forth to see what the shooting was about suddenly yelped and fled as the oncoming panicked loose-stock headed for them down the very centre of the roadway.

Singleton stopped bouncing and rolling, dumbly felt the earth reverberating and despite his temporarily stunned condition, by instinct alone he flopped over looking frantically for shelter. The outlaws were coming directly down upon him, but they were now being fired upon from far back, and they were riding sidewards, loosely and handily, guns in hand, waiting for the possemen to get within handgun range.

For Singleton, who arched his body and dug into the summer-hard dusty earth in order to be positioned for flight, the gunfire did not mean danger until he saw a great gout of gun dust explode five feet to one side. *He was under personal attack!*

There was no weapon in his hipholster. He was not clear-headed and his body had deep pain in it from the fall, but fear and desperation were powerfully motivating factors. He dropped and rolled, kept rolling, and when he saw the outlaws coming directly at him, and also saw the entrance to the alleyway, he sprang up, pain and all, broke into a run and neither looked to his left, where someone was again trying to shoot him, nor farther back where the renegades and possemen were now close enough to brisk up their hand-gun fire, and their wild cursing and shouting as they too raced for the comparative shelter of the alleyway.

Singleton was much closer. He got down there first with his lungs afire and his head clearing enough to help him concentrate upon shelter. There were corrals by the dozen, and there was the rear-opening of the livery-barn. He scuttled towards the barn, and up front someone was also running. It was one of those gunmen looking like loafers Singleton had seen earlier and had just about ignored, only now the 'loafer' had his Winchester up across his body in both hands. He had downed Singleton's horse and now he was concentrating upon doing the same for Singleton.

They almost reached their respective barn-entrances simultaneously, but since Singleton had started earlier, and certainly had the more desperate motivation, he was racing faster and got there first. Even so, as he sprang around the opening and flattened to one side of it as the first of the racing outlaws lunged past, out back in the alleyway, that gunman out front arrived in his front-yard entranceway, dropped to one knee and snugged back the Winchester. Singleton saw, understood, and dropped. The gunman fired. One second later another of those racing outlaws dashed past, out back. He probably did not see the gunman up front, but he most certainly heard the gunshot and knew where it had come from. He swung half around in the saddle and let fly with a wild random shot.

The man up front squawked, jumped to his feet and fled.

Singleton lay in manured dirt looking up there, wishing with all his heart for a sixgun.

The gunfire out back swelled. Singleton did not risk peeking. He lay and sucked great amounts of air into his lungs and felt sweat running like rainwater under his shirt.

The possemen were yelling like bronco-Indians as they too charged down the alley, and out front where those blind-panicky horses were clearing the roadway, and even the plankwalks, there was more yelling.

Then the swirling, running fight was past, on down the back-alley sounding steadily less thunderous, and Singleton propped himself up with both hands, watching the front.

No one came over to that exposed doorway again. But they would, he was sure of that. They would realise he was is there and they would return as soon as the rest of the furious fight got far enough away.

He measured the distance, familiarised himself with the gloomy old log barn's interior, figured where the harness-room was and edged around among the box-stalls along the north wall in an effort to get up there.

He made it, exposed most of the way but with no one evidently willing to rush him from either the front or back. Standing just inside the horse-sweat-scented harness-room he listened as the diminishing sounds of battle continued to sweep on southward, out the lower end of Fletcherville.

Even the bedlam incited by the free-running loose-stock out in the roadway slackened. A temporary lull ensued and Singleton, with a painful side and back, turned to look into the shadows of the tangy-scented room around him.

Harness was draped from high pegs, both chain-harness and leather, both team and buggy harness. There were saddles on inverted V-racks, one atop the other, along with sweat-stiff saddleblankets, and one wall had coffee tins nailed overhead-high for bridles. It was a cluttered room, complete with a filthy old cot, a cast-iron little stove, and a battered desk and chair where, no doubt, the liveryman in his free-time, did his book-work.

There was also an hexagonal-barrelled small calibre double-action rifle leaning in the corner beside the desk, probably for killing the rats which inevitably infested every barn—livery or otherwise—where grain and grain-hay were to be found.

It was a very poor weapon by almost all standards but one. It was better than no weapon at all.

Singleton walked back, grabbed the little thing, returned to the harness-room door to stand and listen, and when he was certain the men he knew perfectly well were still out there would be able to hear, he called forth.

"Hey; you fellers out front! My name is Singleton and I'm not one of the renegades. I'm ..."

The gunshot which came on a vicious angle to shatter the harness-room door where Singleton was standing, had to have been fired by someone close enough to have heard—and disbelieved—what Singleton had just said.

He reeled from wood-splinters, felt his way among the draped harness, and brushed his upper body then gripped the rat-rifle with a cold and furious anger.

"You son of a bitch," he sang out. "I was trying to explain. I'm *not* one of those ... !"

This time there were two of them, one out front, one out back in the alleyway. They fired almost in unison. Lead tore holes in the harness-room wall this time.

Singleton edged farther back, felt genuine fear for the first time, felt trapped in the little harness-room, and eventually felt the kind of desperation a man would have to feel with only one doorway in front of him through which he might escape, and that door was deliberately being watched by men unwilling to listen but who were perfectly willing to kill him.

The silence returned. It remained this time until some horsemen out front in the roadway, evidently returning from their wild pursuit of the fleeing renegades, were greeted by exultant townsmen, one of whom called in a bull-bass voice to warn the riders one of those outlaws sons of bitches was cornered in the livery-barn.

"That one who got his horse shot out from under him north of the alleyway. And be careful, he's as dangerous as a darned snake. Be right careful!"

11

A MATTER OF EVENING THE SCORE

Singleton had time to reflect upon two ironies. One of them had to do with the fact that he had not been unaware of the possibility that, being caught between both sides, he would probably be shot at, and the other irony had to do with Ed Bradley. Just where the hell was he right about now!

A man whistled. It was one of those very loud sounds made by using two fingers in the mouth. Clearly, it was a signal. Singleton inched soundlessly ahead as far as the shattered door and risked a peek.

For a while he saw nothing, then a wisp of dark movement snagged his attention, but by the time he got turned westerly in the direction of the rear-alley, the silhouette was gone. Singleton thought the man had rushed from south to north, in the alley, then it occurred to him that the man might have sped from the south *into* the barn, then to shelter among the stalls back in the gloom along the north wall.

One thing he was sure of, with that little rat-rifle he was in no position to challenge someone carrying a Colt and a Winchester.

He tried to call out again, but this time, with two previous experiences to convince him of the value of being very careful, he moved back as deep into the little room as possible before yelling.

"Listen, damn it! I'm not one of those outlaws! I was riding with them because ... !"

This time, there were not two gunmen out there in front, there were at least four of them and they were at both ends of the barn when they cut loose. A blind bullet came through, broke a harness-peg, and a great amount of heavy old chain-harness fell noisily into a hopeless heap.

Evidently this sound had carried because a man's harsh voice said, "I think we got him. I heard what seemed like a feller fallin' into the harness and draggin' it off the hook as he fell with it."

A less excited voice dryly said, "All right, Elbert, you heard it. You walk in there and see."

Nothing more was said and for a while there was no fresh indication that the closing-up ring of possemen out there even existed, but Singleton had no illlusions about that. He was huddling in a smelly little room which was being systematically riddled around him.

He swore about Ed Bradley and he swore about the county sheriff. Both of them had to be out there, somewhere; at least if most of the other possemen had returned to town it certainly seemed logical to expect those men to have also returned, and not a thing was being done to extricate Singleton from a situation which he came to increasingly believe was only going to end one way unless he got out of that harness-room, and also out of the liverybarn, if it were possible to do so.

He crept to the doorway, got down prone and inched his head out, looking for that man who had slipped inside from out back.

He saw nothing. There was a stall door ajar mid-way along the dark north wall, though, and because he was attuned to total clarity and total recall, he did not remember any of those doors being open when he had earlier felt his way along them to reach the harness-room.

He bleakly reflected, then eased the rat-rifle forward. if he had been able to detachedly view himself right at this moment, he would have shuddered. A man in his right mind should know better than to attempt what he had in mind. Of course, a man in his right mind probably would not be found inside a shot-up log liverybarn, either.

He inched his body ahead a little, got the rifle up one-handed, covered the open stall door, and gathered both legs up beneath himself, slowly. When he was ready to risk it, he soundlessly rose, soundlessly looked up front and saw no one, took a deep-down breath and stepped out of the harness-room into the perpetually gloomy liverybarn runway. He held his breath one second, then swung and hurriedly headed for that opened stall door.

With the rat-rifle raised, one-handed, he had almost made it when someone out back in the alley risked a peek, saw a wispy silhouette moving along the stall-fronts, and yelped.

Another man would probably have taken aim and fired. As it was the startled posseman who called forth did not make an attempt to fire, he was content simply to warn his friends.

Singleton had at most three seconds. All his adversaries out there had to do was fling up their guns, lean a fraction until they could see, then start firing.

But there was one very serious drawback. The men outside were sitting in brilliant sunshine. When they eased over to peer down inside the log barn where it was gloomily dark, their eyes were unable to make an instantaneous adjustment. One of them fired but the bullet got no farther than a swinging saddle-pole.

The other men were straining with pinched-down eyes to see, and Singleton pitched away caution, sprang into the cell, saw the crouching man up by the west wall with his fisted Colt, and fired his rat-rifle with one hand. It made a little waspish sound. The man with the Colt in his fist twisted so suddenly he nearly lost his balance.

Maybe he was a storekeeper of some kind, or maybe he was a bartender, but whatever his vocation he was not a seasoned gunman, otherwise he would have been holding a *cocked* gun. Now, as he stumbled, regained his balance and swung to shoot Singleton, he had to fatally delay and haul back the dog with a thumb-pad.

Singleton needed no more time than that to roar a savage curse and swing forward with the rat-rifle rising like a spear. He jabbed the posseman in the middle, the man made a gasp and a desperate leap. Singleton swung

the rat-rifle like a club, and missed.
The posseman was half-turned away
as he got his weapon cocked. He was
turning back when Singleton hurled
the rat-rifle and came in right behind
it, both balled fists swinging. He
connected, hard, and the posseman's
gun exploded into the overhead roof.

Singleton bored in swinging. He
had no particuar skill and certainly
no finesse, but he had desperation,
which was occasionally a suitable
alternative when the opponent was no
better equipped.

The posseman was larger than
Singleton and older, but he never got
a chance to demonstrate whether he
was Singleton's match or not because
his attacker did not allow him an
opportunity to do anything but raise
both arms to protect his face and
upper body.

Singleton went after the posseman
hammer and tongs; every vestige of
fury Singleton had felt lately, along

with his fears and his desperation drove him on, punching with arms like muscular pistons.

He battered the posseman along the west stall-wall, punched and slammed him into a corner, pawed to get past the man's guard, then stepped back and kicked high. He connected at the posseman's belt-buckle and the man cried out hoarsely, dropped his arms and doubled over in pain.

Singleton reached, positioned the man and fired his right fist from the shoulder. The posseman went backwards, bounced off the log wall and toppled forward to land belly-down and unmoving.

Singleton groped by, stepping across the man until he found that Colt. Never in his life had a sixgun felt so satisfying in his grip.

Out front a man called into the barn, making an echo. "Hey

Singleton! That you down in there?
This is Ed Bradley!"

Singleton closed his hand around
the wonderfully reassuring walnut
stock of the sixgun and moved to the
stall door.

"Prove it!" he yelled back.

For five seconds Ed Bradley must
have been nonplussed, before he
appreciated Singleton's scepticism
and called out again.

"We got one of them—a young
feller who died grinning his idiotic
head off. There's some fellers with
Sheriff Flannery scouring the range
south-west of town for the others.
Singleton ... ?"

"Walk down in here where I can
see you, Bradley!"

The constable obeyed, but as he
entered the barn he used a placating
tone of voice to announce his arrival.
"I came back as quick as I dared,
Singleton. I figured the folks around

here might not believe you wasn't one of those renegades."

Bradley halted near the harness-room and stared in disbelief at the shot-up interior and the splintered door.

Singleton leaned, recognised his companion from Cutbank, and said, "I ought to blow your gawddamned head off! Why in hell did you let those darned fools get behind them instead of in front? They darned near got me killed."

Singleton walked forth, holstering the appropriated Colt. He jerked his head. "There's a local hero knocked senseless in that stall."

Out front a craggy-looking towns-man with a carbine held up across his body two-handedly, looked and sang out.

"You all right down there, Con-stable?"

Singleton turned, saw this man, remembered the way the man who had originally tried to kill him had held his Winchester in the precise same fashion, and turned to stroll forward as Ed Bradley answered the man.

"Yeah, I'll be all right. There's one of your fellers in a stall down here knocked out. That man approaching you—that's Singleton, the feller I told you I thought was cornered in here."

Ed turned and also started towards the yonder tree-shaded yard, but he did not get up there soon enough, probably because he had no more idea anything was going to happen than did that craggy individual with the squinting no-quarter eyes and the craggy features, standing with his carbine up across his body.

Singleton did not say a word. He walked to within three feet of that townsman, reached with his left hand to slightly push aside the Winchester and fired his right fist with blinding speed and back-breaking power. The Winchester-man went backwards in a pin-wheeling fall which did not stop completely until he had slid on his back a good four feet, and he was a heavy individual. Blood flowed from his smashed mouth.

There were three stunned townsmen out there, too nonplussed even to raise their guns. Bradley squawked and ran ahead.

"What in hell are you doing!" he demanded, blocking Singleton's access to the other possemen.

"That son of a bitch tried to shoot me fifteen minutes ago," exclaimed Singleton. "He never even so much as gave me a chance to raise my arms. He dropped to his knee and tried to kill me."

One of the other townsmen finally recovered and indignantly said, "Gawddammit, how was we to know?"

Singleton rested his right hand

upon the walnut gunstock in his holster. "And which one of you bastards shot my horse?" he snarled.

12

MEN AND EVENTS

The excitement throughout Fletcherville resulting from the sudden and
deafeningly violent running gunfight
between Sheriff Houston Flannery
with his possemen, and those hard-
riding four outlaws, was somewhat
dampened when the townsmen and
returned-possemen met along the bar-
fronts to re-hash what had happened
at the liverybarn. The man out front
with the carbine in his hands, had a
broken jaw. The posseman down in
the horse-stall had a .22 calibre bullet
in his upper right shoulder, had a
purple bruise where he had been

kicked in the stomach, and had a broken front tooth.

It was being said that those two manhunters from up north at Cutbank were worse than a pair of bloody-hand bronco-bucks on a war trail.

Two townsmen were down at the jailhouse with Singleton and Bradley. One of them was a former lawman whose name was Kandelin and the other townsman was a bare-knuckle fighter from San Francisco who had settled in Fletcherville two years earlier, when he had married a local girl. Those were the only two willing to go down where Bradley and Singleton had taken up residence after leaving the shot-up liverybarn.

The former lawman showed sagacity; he brought with him an unopened bottle of malt whisky and several shot-glasses. Now, the four of them sat in there, allowing their agitation to atrophy gradually as they talked and sipped.

Singleton was still sulphurous. "That silly bastard out front," he said to the others, "got off light. When a man shoots at you, every place I've ever been they shoot back."

The pugilist nodded a cropped head. Little eyes peered from deep inside mounds of scar-tissue. "Sure. Me too," he agreed. "Except that the dumb idiot didn't know you wasn't one of them renegades."

"He had a tongue didn't he?" asked Singleton, leaning for the former lawman to solemnly refill his shot-glass. "I tried to tell them and no—they wanted my topknot. I should have shot him instead of hitting him."

The former lawman leaned back holding aloft a glass of amber liquid. "Mister Singleton; if you'd shot him, we'd have been after you like Houston Flannery is after those outlaws."

The lawman lowered his glass, drank from it while gazing steadily over the rim, then he said, "I know exactly how you feel."

They'd all been saying this, including Ed Bradley. Singleton did not believe any one of them understood how he felt. "Listen to me," he exclaimed. "This lousy town owes me one hell of a good horse. I rode that animal an awful lot of miles over the past three or four years, and he never balked, never got sick, never offered to bite or strike or kick."

The pugilist rolled his eyes around, and settled them upon Bradley, but the constable from Cutbank was having no part of this conversation. He was busily cleaning his sixgun with rags and a rammer found atop the sheriff's desk. He went right ahead with his work and hardly even looked up.

A grizzled, weathered-looking rangeman poked his head in, leaned to look quizzically around, then said, "I just come from Hap Webster, gents. He says someone taken his sixgun off the floor of that cell where someone knocked him out and he wants his gun back."

The pugilist and former lawman gazed irritably at this intruder without either of them uttering a sound. Singleton turned, ready to respond, but Ed Bradley beat him to it.

"Partner, you better pull your head back and close that door, or you're likely to get up in the morning with a third eye in the centre of your darned forehead. *Move!*"

The cowboy moved. He sucked back and slammed the door after himself, and he did it so swiftly even the unsmiling former lawman came near to grinning. The pugilist smiled, looked at Singleton and said, "It's not bad whisky, is it?"

Singleton lifted his glass to make

the test. When he lowered it he loosened, slumped in the chair and slowly let his breath out. "No, it's not bad," he conceded, using a changing tone. "Where's that stuffed-shirt of a sheriff?"

The former lawman took exception. "Wait a darned minute. Houston Flannery has served this community right well for six years now, and when he's up for election come the summer after next, folks hereabouts will show their appreciation, by golly. They know a good man when they ..."

"Oh for Chris'sake," rumbled Singleton, and arose to turn and face Bradley. "Are we going to set here listening to this crap, or are we going to finish what we started out to do?"

Bradley looked a little apologetically in the direction of the townsmen, arose and wordlessly followed Singleton outside.

They were two-thirds of the way to

the liverybarn where a little group of arm-waving and loudly talking individuals were standing in afternoon shadows, before Bradley said, "If we overtake Sheriff Flannery you'd better be in a different mood, Singleton." He did not say what that mood should be, he instead walked ahead under the gape-mouth stares of those townsmen in the shade, and looked into the barn to ascertain whether or not there was a dayman around.

There was. He came forth from the ruined harness-room looking harassed and upset. When he squinted into the yard sunlight and recognised the pair of men walking down to ask for a pair of livery horses, the hostler forgot to momentarily breathe. He forced a weak smile.

"Can I help you, gents?"

"Two good stout saddlehorses, rigged out," replied Ed.

The hostler's head bobbed up and

down like an apple on a string, then he fled into the deeper areas of the old building, and those men out front began to edge over a little closer in order to be able to hear, but Singleton was not in a very talkative frame of mind, and that left Bradley with the choice of talking to himself or not talking at all.

Finally, though, as he rolled and lighted a smoke, Singleton said, "We should have borrowed a pair of Winchesters from the sheriff's wall-rack."

Bradley was more sanguine. "By the time we find Flannery he'll have them tied to their horses, dead or alive."

The liveryman came forth leading two big strong young animals and as he cross-tied them for saddling he said, "How do they look, gents? These are two of our best animals. Well-broke and stout."

Singleton studied the pair of horses without comment. Bradley assured the hostler the animals would be satisfactory, and ten minutes later as they were walking the horses out front, past those curious idlers, someone at the lower end of town called out. In the distance, south of town and slightly to the west, a clutch of horsemen were coming all in a little bunch. One of those men in the liverybarn yard said it was probably Houston Flannery but another man, closer to the roadway and therefore better able to see, said he didn't think so because Flannery had departed with about fifteen possemen, of which only three or four had returned, and that bunch out yonder did not amount to that many men.

Singleton's mood was still unpleasant. He turned his livery horse and swung up over leather as he called to Ed Bradley to come along.

They struck out down the main thoroughfare, which ensured that they would ultimately encounter the approaching riders. Neither of them were particularly interested until, almost at the lower end of Fletcherville where they saw the horsemen coming directly at them up the stage-road, it began to appear that whoever they were, these strangers had decided to take an interest in Bradley and Singleton. They were blocking the road as they came on, and they were doing it deliberately.

Ed drew rein and sat in the centre of the road, waiting. Singleton stopped also, and loosened that appropriated sixgun he was wearing, but it turned out not to be that kind of an encounter.

The foremost of those five horsemen was florid-faced, grey, thick and large. He looked to be perhaps sixty or sixty-five years old. He also was dressed well and rode a good outfit, which to most rangemen, meant 'cow*man*' not 'cow*boy*'. This time it did indeed mean that. When the strange riders stopped, that older man spoke briskly, without smiling, and straight to the point. He said, "Good day, gents. I'm Stan Kegley of S-back-to-back. I had a rider shot and killed about an hour ago by strangers. Before I let you pass I'd like to know who you are."

Singleton answered. His slowly diminishing anger was finally diluted enough. He bobbed his head at his companion. "He's town constable up at Cutbank. His name is Ed Bradley. My name is Singleton. We came down here on the trail of four renegades being led by a man named Foster. Right now we're on our way to go look for them—and for Sheriff Flannery who is on their trail."

Bradley asked about the killing of the S-back-to-back rider and that brusque older man answered forthrightly. "All we know is that he was on our east range, coming in. The rest of us were in the yard and heard a flurry of gunfire."

Singleton held up a hand. "Did they take his horse?"

"Yes. Shot him three times and took his outfit."

"What did they leave in its stead?"

The cowman didn't know because they had only gone out as far as they had to in order to locate their dead man. Then Stan Kegley said, "You two are going out, right now?" and before he was answered he also said, "All right, gents. We'll just turn around and go right along with you."

Ed Bradley did not appear to object, but his companion did. "We appreciate the offer," Singleton told Kegley, "but this here is a sort of personal thing with me." He lifted his rein-hand, touched his hatbrim to old Kegley, ignored the looks of the other rangemen around Kegley and eased the livery horse onward.

He got fifty or sixty yards before

Ed caught up. Bradley had explained as best he could, back there, and now as he rejoined Singleton he looped reins and rolled a smoke without saying a word until he was inhaling, and exhaling.

"You got a hell of a disposition," he announced.

Singleton looked down his nose. "How am I supposed to feel? That bunch of idiotic bastards back there killed my horse and tried their best to kill me."

"Well hell, they didn't know who you were, out there on the range with Foster and those other renegades."

"And where were you," demanded Singleton, beginning to get fired up all over again. "Why in hell didn't you and Flannery stay out where you could see who was leading them on in? For a fact, Bradley, where *were* you?"

The Cutbank constable considered the glowing tip of his cigarette before answering. He did not give the impression that he particularly wanted to say anything.

"Flannery's a strange feller," he said, by way of prefacing less charitable statements. "Well; when I got down here and busted in on him at the jailhouse, told him how we'd set up those renegades, he got mad because we didn't tell him first so's he could be out there too." Bradley smoked a moment. "Thing is, he don't like other folks taking initiative in his bailiwick."

"What in the hand-made hell," exclaimed Singleton, his tone ringing with disgust, "was we supposed to do: Break off out there, run back to town to tell Flannery what was happening, then run back out there?"

Bradley blew out a big breath. "All I can tell you is that he said he'd get up a posse and corral the outlaws without you or me, and when I told him where you'd be—out front baiting them along—he said he wasn't interested in where you'd be, and he stamped out of his office ... So I went up the road looking out yonder for some sign of you, didn't see any and headed for the saloon to see if I could round up a few fellers to lend me a hand, and the next thing I knew there was gunfire. When I ran out front I saw the renegades busting down the back alley over yonder, so I sprinted southward to try and help intercept them."

"Where was Flannery and his possemen?"

"Below town on the east side of the stage-road where they expected the renegades to bust out—only they turned westerly, so they got a good half-mile start before Flannery even got going." Bradley dropped his smoke. "I'll tell you the truth, Singleton. He may be the best lawmen they've had down here, and folks may think he's the greatest, but between the two of us I've owned dogs who were smarter. All Flannery's got is a mile-high idea of his own importance."

Singleton looked at Bradley, then he glanced behind, back in the direction of town, and finally as he settled forward he looked left and right and dead ahead. There was no sign of a posse, or men being pursued, in any direction.

"The damned fool probably ran them out of the country," he told Bradley. "And that means I got to start over again."

13

INTO THE ROCKS!

Singleton was wrong. At first Ed Bradley was the only one of them to hear it—the very faint and very distant sound of gunfire. In fact it did not actually appear as a discernible sound as much as it appeared as a shock-wave, as a kind of undulating reverberation travelling through the clear air more as a break in the atmospheric continuum than as an actual sound—more echo than gunblast.

Ed rode a half-mile straining to hear. He said nothing until he was certain, then he stopped his horse and held his hand up for Singleton to also rein up.

They heard the definite sounds, finally, and Singleton turned to look in the direction from which they were coming. After a speculative moment he said, "Cornered; someone's cornered and under attack."

They loped the livery mounts without great haste. As they rode overland they also kept a careful watch. But wherever those battlers were, they certainly were a long way off because excepting a few little bosques of oaks all this lower-down range country was grassland without very much shelter.

They had the general area fixed in their minds long before the gunfire abruptly ceased. Somewhere to the south-west, and in fact considerably more westerly than Singleton and Bradley might otherwise have explored in their manhunt, over where the territory looked to be more rugged, more rocky and more undulating with more tree-cover, was where they thought the cornered men were trying to fight off their foemen.

It never for a moment occurred to Singleton that they might not be riding down-country to reinforce the law in its fight with outlaws driven to ground.

Not even when Ed Bradley finally raised a pointing arm and said, "In that belt of big black boulders yonder," and Singleton could finally make out some tied horses farther back.

He hardly more than glanced at the tethered saddle-stock. His interest was focused upon that belt of boulders. It looked to cover perhaps ten or fifteen acres, with some rocks piled like battlements, one atop the others. The entire area was evidently an ancient lava-flow, with huge black-stone boulders as large as a mounted man embedded in the underground schist. It was anyone's guess where that stone had come from; the nearest high peak which could have been a prehistoric volcano was at least five miles distant, to the south. Someday people would accept the possibility of an explosion that violent, but to Singleton and Bradley, even if they'd dwelt upon rocks as large as houses being shot five miles through the air, this was not the time to be interested in how that rock belt was formed, it was the time to slacken gait and to begin a far-out encircling movement going half-way around the rock-field in order to get some idea of exactly what was in progress up there.

What they eventually encountered, out behind the black-stone battlements was a little band of grazing horses, with whitish dried sweat on their backs and sides. They rode closer, got as near as they could before the horses began bunching up

to flee, and Singleton pointed,
"Arapahoe horses."

Bradley was not surprised. He
twisted to glance in the direction of
the rock-field, which was quiet now.
"They'll be holed up in there, and
from the looks of it I'd say it'll take a
howitzer to blow them out."

Singleton kept studying the horses.
"A smart man would round up that
remuda, turn back and keep right on
going until he was back up at Cutbank."

Bradley squinted. "You want to do
that, then?"

"Nope. I said that's what a smart
feller would do. I'm not a smart
feller. Besides, I got to see to it that
those renegades get settled up with."

He turned his horse and considered
the rock-field. "Where do you suppose Sheriff Flannery is?"

Bradley made a casual, wide
gesture. "Around front, I'd guess."

They turned and started back the

way they had come, covered perhaps two hundred yards and were passing close to some jack-pines growing out of the edge of the rock-belt when several carbines blasted away. For fifty or sixty feet Singleton was certain the cornered outlaws and the Fletcherville possemen were resuming their battle. He rode a few feet, happened to be glancing at the jack-pines and saw a fist-sized piece of bark suddenly detach itself and go flying out into the grass.

He reacted instinctively by kicking loose both feet and hurling himself down the side of the astonished livery horse.

He yelled at Ed Bradley that they were under personal attack. Ed did not wait, he also bailed out and rolled frantically into the bosque of trees. Ed left his hat out in the grass and for a long while made no effort to recover it.

Other gunmen joined the firing,

and this time it appeared that the besiegers and the besieged were resuming their earlier fight. For a while Singleton and Bradley, side by side in among the spindly little worthless trees had nothing more than puffs of soiled gunsmoke to give them clues where men were firing. There were no sightings of the individuals themselves until Singleton caught sight of someone in the rocks. He waited and watched, saw this man twice, and nudged Bradley.

"Watch that slab-rock to our right beyond the tallest pinnacle. There's a feller in there with a light grey hat."

Bradley jerked around for a look, then said, "Light grey hat?"

It struck Singleton at the same moment. *None of those renegades had been wearing a light grey hat!*

Bradley suddenly said, "I'll be damned. That's not the renegades holed up in the rocks, that's Flannery and his riders from Fletcherville."

Singleton had difficulty accepting this. "You said he had about ten men with him."

"He did have. When I turned back to go lookin' for you, three or maybe four other men also started back, but that left him with at least ten other fellers."

"Then how in hell can four renegades be holding him in those rocks?" demanded Singleton, straining to see more than just the smoke-puffs.

A bullet came from nowhere to slash its way through the jack-pines nearby with a meaty sound. Singleton ducked low and remained that way, moving just his eyes in an effort to locate the sniper firing at their hiding-place. He found no one, decided it could have simply been wild shot, and raised up just enough for the next slug to shower dust and pebbles in his face. It apparently was no accident that second time, and

Singleton got flat down as he wiped his face, thinking that it hadn't been an accident the first time, either.

That same man who had fired on them when they had first come into sight, moving back around from the rear of the stone-field, was probably still trying to shoot them.

Otherwise, though, everyone else seemed fiercely engaged in the sporadic gunfight over in the front of the belt of rocks.

Bradley put his arm up and moved it, but he drew no gunfire. He next tried exposing a leg, pulling it back and easing it forward again. He still drew no gunfire. In fact, those duellists out front where the majority of the gunfire had been coming from, were easing off again. This made Bradley say, "I couldn't locate him, but I'd guess he's gone back round where his friends are."

Singleton had lost part of his interest in this aspect of the fight, and was frowning as he pondered that other aspect, the one where it seemed the possemen were bottled up and under attack by the besieging renegades.

"It don't make a lick of sense for ten men to be driven to the ground by four men, Bradley, and it don't make sense for those ten men to just lie back there in the rocks and not push the fight to those other fellers."

Apparently it made sense to the constable. "I can tell you one thing," he stated. "I don't give a darn if there was a hundred and fifty possemen in those lousy rocks, three or four good men in the right places, could keep the hundred and fifty from coming out of those rocks."

Singleton shied away from disputing this and said, "But how the hell did they get that sheriff and his riders in there to start with?"

Bradley said, "That's not what we got to worry about."

Singleton nodded his head while peering out where the raging battle of moments earlier had died down until there were only an occasional gunshot, and an even more less frequent reply from back in the rocks.

They studied the terrain trying to guess where each renegade was hiding. In the end Singleton said, "They'll keep moving. They'll shoot then move. But there's not a hell of a lot of cover if they move very far." He considered the distance for a while, then tapped Bradley's arm. "I think we can crawl around to the rear of the rock-field, and slip in there, if we're damned awful careful."

Bradley was not enthusiastic. "Go ahead and get us killed," he muttered, and began edging back in order to be in a position to safely get up to his feet. "There's one of them out front of the rocks who knows we're over here. Remember that."

But Singleton's idea was to withdraw deeper among the spindly jack-pines, until they were completely hidden, then to move around to their left, keep moving in that direction until they were well around the rock-field and out of sight of the man who had been firing at them. From there, he was sure they could get into the rocks because the intervening distance between where they would be and the nearest big boulders, was not more than twenty or thirty yards. For that long, they would be exposed.

It did not occur to either of them that the moment they charged forth into the rocks the defenders in there might consider them as enemies, but that is what happened.

They made it without difficulty to the farthest area of jack-pines and stealthily crept up to the final edge of their protective shelter, hesitated to look across the open territory they now had to cross, and Singleton was encouraged because from this place they could not see the renegades around front, which meant the renegades probably could not see them either. He even tightly smiled when he glanced around at Bradley.

"How good a sprinter are you?" he asked, and the constable grinned back when he replied. "Depends on just how scairt I am, and I got a feelin' I'm going to be scairt."

They ran. Singleton broke from shelter and sped along as hard as he could, which was not very fast but for a man who had not done anything like this in a very long while and who was, as Ed Bradley had suggested, powerfully motivated to get across into the rocks, it was good enough time.

They both got into the first jumble of black-rock boulders and threw themselves down back there. Five seconds later when they were beginning to recover from wildly beating hearts, someone *within* the rock-field opened up on their hiding-place. This time it was not just one Winchester-man. it seemed for a moment as though Sheriff Flannery's entire posse was trying to kill them.

They flattened against gravelly soil back there, in no immediate danger, not even from ricocheting lead, but not feeling safe either, and Singleton turned to make a comment.

"This is the damndest country I was ever in. By gawd the ones we're fixin' to help are trying to do it to me again."

He had to raise his voice, but moments later when the fusillade diminished, as they all seemed to do within a short period of time, he could speak normally.

"I'd like to punch Flannery in the nose."

Ed ignored that, got a peek from between two huge rocks and pulled back slowly. "I think we're being stalked. Sure as hell they figure we're some of Foster's lads."

"If they can count, by gawd, they'd ought to be able to figure that if there's two of us back here, and still four up in front of them ..."

"Three," corrected Bradley. "That grinning, younger one got shot off his horse in the chase from town. That leaves only three of them."

Singleton reverted to an earlier source of disgust. "Three lousy renegades holing up ten possemen and a county sheriff!"

Bradley peeked out again, then confirmed it; they were being stalked by two possemen from up in the forward rocks!

14

MATTERS OF STRATEGY

Singleton remained prone, waiting and watching. When he guessed where those men were who were creeping soundlessly towards the boulders which were shielding him and the Cutbank constable, he gestured and said, "Sneak to the right. I'll go round to the left."

Ed was willing, since remaining where they were was only going to subject them to fresh peril.

Singleton, without a Winchester against men who did have, should perhaps have felt his inferior fire-power, but he hadn't since arriving near the rock-field and he did not feel

that way now, as he slithered snake-
like in an attempt to flank one of
those possemen.

He felt just about as much enmity
towards the possemen as he had for-
merly felt for the renegades and
possibly that helped when he finally
saw someone's spurred, booted foot
slowly draw in out of sight behind
some rocks.

He raised his sixgun, waited until
the man moved again, then cut loose.
Dust and razor-bits of rock erupted in
a thin slot between two rocks, and a
man hunched instinctively and jumped, then flopped and covered his
face.

Singleton hardly raised his voice.
"Stand up and leave your gun down
there!"

The man did not entirely obey; he
got onto both knees like a supplicant
and dug at his face and eyes. That
bombardment of sharp stones had
scratched and lacerated him. He

could not see for a moment or two, and that alone would probably have been demoralising enough, but being flanked, exposed and under someone's gun did the rest.

He said, "That's enough, for Chris'sake!"

Singleton went down to him, growled at him to get down and sat down in the rocks with him. When the posseman could wipe enough water from his eyes with a bandanna to see his captor he peered through swimming tears without a shred of recognition.

Singleton heard someone approaching, guessed it would be Ed, and eased around until he could peer out. He had guessed right. Bradley came forward, wigwagged with a gun-hand when he saw Singleton, then came on with less caution.

The prisoner was down to blinking and sniffing. His eyes had evidently not been genuinely damaged by that explosion of tallis particles in front of him. But he had for a while been terrified over the prospect of having impaired vision.

He blinked rapidly in Bradley's direction. "You're that feller from Cutbank," he exclaimed, and looked at Singleton. "Is this feller with you?"

Ed did not answer. "Where's Flannery?"

The injured man shook his head sideways to indicate the farther-back big boulder-field. "We thought you was more outlaws," he explained, indifferently signalling an answer to Ed's question. "Someone seen you fellers come up, and said you was with them outlaws."

"Wrong," stated Singleton. "We were trying to help you fellers ... Tell us something. How the hell can three lousy renegades keep all you possemen in those rocks like you was a herd of children?"

The possemen raised his bandanna to the injured eyes again as he answered that. "They caught us flat-footed. Did you see them horses back across the open country a ways? Well; those are our animals. Sheriff Flannery said he was sure them renegades was over here in these rocks, so we left our horses over yonder and commenced stalking ahead and when we got close enough to be concentratin' real hard on sneakin' undetected into the rocks ..."

"Oh hell," said Singleton in great disgust. "The darned renegades weren't ever in the rocks, they were back yonder hiding in the area about where you left the saddle-stock."

"Right," exlaimned the town-posseman. "But they couldn't run off with our animals because as soon as they tried it and we saw 'em, we opened up and drove them to the ground. That's what it's been about ever since; them tryin' to get away with our saddle-stock to set us afoot, and us in the rocks firin' at ever' man out there who exposes himself even a little."

Singleton turned and gazed at Bradley. Neither of them said anything for a moment, then Bradley addressed their captive upon a matter which had not been under discussion. "You know the feller who was stalking us with you a few minutes ago?"

"Yeah. Jack Carruthers."

"Sing out," commanded Ed Bradley. "Call him over here."

The prisoner obeyed. He called several times before there was any response, and eventually the second stalker came into the little stone-ring where the three men were sitting. He too recognised Constable Bradley and looked askance at Singleton.

It only required a few minutes to tell Carruthers what had been revealed to his companion, then he was invited to sit down.

Elsewhere, the stubborn little Mexican stand-off was still bitterly in progress. Each time a renegade would dare show himself in an attempt to untie the posse horses, a watcher in the rocks would drive him back.

It was not the fight Bradley and Singleton had thought. In fact, as Singleton hunched there looking, listening, and reflecting, his judgement confirmed his earlier assessment of that conceited sheriff. Houston Flannery, like most people of monumental ego, was a fool. Right at this juncture, though, all that really meant was that Flannery had got all of them into a very deadly situation.

He said, "You fellers go back. Now you darned well listen to me. You go back and tell that horse's-butt of a sheriff of yours Constable Bradley and I'll make a big sashay—real big—and try and come in from the west where we can get a chance at those renegades—and if Flannery tells you dimwits to open up when the fight starts between us and those outlaws—you tell him I'm going to shoot him on sight." Singleton looked from man to man. "I owe the son of a bitch for darned near getting me killed back in town. If he does that again, so help me, I'll pay him right up to the gullet. 'You remember all that?"

The man with the watering eyes answered curtly. "We'll tell him." Then he also said, "Mister; I don't think just the pair of you can bust those renegades."

Singleton was unimpressed by this. "I'd be surprised as hell if you did think so," he said tartly. "Ten of you and three renegades—I'd be surprised as hell if you thought two men could do anything at all ... Let's go, Ed."

They had to retrace their steps, leaving the troubled possemen, but when they reached that strip where they had been able to bolt tree-shelter to the rocks, and where they now had to reverse that process, Bradley dropped behind a pinnacle and hissed for Singleton to do likewise.

Bradley jutted his jaw. "Watch."

A wisp of shadowy movement over yonder showed from moment to moment as someone, carrying a Winchester in one fist, was soundlessly and stealthily creeping southward, evidently either tracking Singleton and Bradley, or paralleling their earlier route.

Bradley was impressed. "They got guts. You got to hand that to them. Only two fellers are over yonder by the horses, if that's one of them over yonder."

Singleton gauged the distance. It was too great for accurate sixgunfire. On the other hand, sixguns made a lot more noise than carbines, and to someone who had already been under fire, just the gunblast would be unnerving. At least he made that guess as he waited for the shadow to show itself again, moving in and out among the spindly jack-pines, and when he saw the shadow he said, "Let's go," jumped up and raced dead ahead, firing as he charged.

The man in among the jack-pines was unprepared for an attack. He had not in fact been tracking Bradley and Singleton at all. He had not even found their horses in among the jack-pines because he had not gone any deeper than the nearest fringe of trees. His objective had been to sneak in behind the possemen, open up with a furious blast of gunfire and divert them until his two companions out yonder could cut the tethers and stampede the posse's saddle-stock.

Now, seeing two men with blazing hand-guns charging directly at him, he turned, unnerved, and tried to flee. Bradley caught him in the lower leg with a lucky shot, and as the man went down he lost his Winchester.

Bradley sprang up and leaned, cocked gun aimed at the writhing man's face. That broken leg had already drained the fight out of him. He gritted his teeth, held his bleeding leg with both hands and rocked back and forth.

Singleton came up, kicked the Winchester away, stooped and yanked free the man's holstered Colt, tossed it backwards and said. "Sam, you bastard, you're lucky it's only your leg."

The tall, lanky outlaw did not appear to have heard Singleton, he had his jaws locked and his eyes pinched so tightly closed there were tears being squeezed out. The leg was excruciatingly painful, Singleton could appreciate that, but at this moment Singleton was fresh out of sympathy. He knelt, shook Sam by the shoulder and said, "Which one of you shot the little Indian girl in the back of the head?"

Sam did not answer, did not seem even to have heard, so Singleton bore down with his powerful grip on Sam's shoulder, kept right on bearing down until the outlaw tried to wrench away, then Singleton repeated the question.

Sam, who never looked directly at people other than his outlaw companions, kept his contorted face averted, but he spoke, and Singleton's vice-grip loosened a little.

"Hank. Hank shot the pup. Me'n Ace, we took on the buck when he come walkin' into the clearing. We riddled him. Jesus! This leg is killing me!"

Singleton remained unsympathetic. "Who shot the woman?"

"Juniper."

Singleton looked momentarily blank. "Who?"

"Tom Juniper, the 'breed. He

knew about things like that; he knew
there'd be a squaw in the tipi so he
run over, poked his head inside and
shot her as she was pawing through
some skins for a carbine."

Singleton regarded the injured
man thoughtfully. "I hope you're
lyin'; then I'll be justified in coming
back for you."

He arose, looked at Bradley who
was returning from retrieving the
injured man's weapons. Bradley
shrugged. They had nothing to tie the
injured outlaw with, but it did not
seem very likely that he could go far,
crawling on all fours.

Bradley turned and led the way
back through the trees towards the
area where he had last seen those two
livery horses.

The sporadic gunfire up ahead was
still occasionally erupting, and just
before they got to the horses Bradley
said, "Stubborn damned fools, that's
what those outlaws are. Sooner or

later someone is going to come up the coach-road, or more riders'll be coming down this way from Fletcherville ... I'll tell you something about outlaws. The minute they stop moving, stop manoeuvring back and forth so's folks can't get a decent fix on their position, they're goners."

Singleton was walking towards the horses when he said, "Save it."

Moments later when they had the animals in tow and were leading them along the far-back area of jack-pines, the gunfire up front stopped altogether. Singleton quickened his pace, and eventually turned to spring up over leather and urge the livery horse ahead. He worried for fear the outlaws had finally freed those tethered posse-horses. If that happened, of course Flannery and his possemen would be left on foot far behind, which would mean that Singleton and Bradley would be the only pursuers able to offer mounted pursuit.

But when they got to the far fringe of trees they could see that the tethered horses were still out there.

Bradley had made a rapid assessment and called sharply as he turned almost directly northward.

There was only one way for the pair of them to get clear of the jack-pines without being seen as they did it, and that was to ride northward. In fact northward and eastward so that the jack-pines would screen them from the outlaws around to the south-west.

It would mean miles of diversionary riding, but there was no other choice.

15

BOLD MEN

Time, which was of some value under all circumstances, was the first neglected element when men were in active defence of their lives or were in single-minded pursuit of enemies.

Singleton did not once glance skyward to get some idea of the time of day when Bradley led their withdrawal from the jack-pine area. He knew it was going to take time to get far enough away from the area where those contending men were locked in their stubborn fight, but his concern was only with trying to make as good time as possible in flanking the renegades, in seeking to reach an area west of them, and the posse-horses, where it would be possible to open a fresh attack.

He was thinking exclusively in terms of getting around to the west. He was not reflecting upon the time of day it was.

Ed Bradley was probably doing the same thing because as he led their overland ride he kept alternating between a kidney-jolting trot and a decent horseman's little mile-eating lope, and Ed had already fixed in his mind a point towards which he was aiming.

Singleton rolled a smoke, relaxed a little, said nothing and turned from time to time in an effort to stay oriented in the vast emptiness across which they were presently riding.

He found no fault at all with the way Bradley chose to cover the distance. By the time they had covered so much ground Ed could begin curving back around so as to start their inward approach from the west, although they had been a long time on the trail it did not seem so to Singleton, who now began riding upright in his stirrups trying to make out the familiar landmarks they had abandoned more than an hour earlier.

Eventually, when he could see the black pinnacles again, he could also orient himself to the north and south. He knew, for example, where the posse-horses were, and from there, he could surmise with fair accuracy about where the remaining renegades would be.

He paused to speculate about Sam. He decided that Hank Foster and the 'breed named Tom Juniper would by this time be worried about Sam, who had had plenty of time to get into position behind the possemen and start his diversionary gunfire. Clearly, Sam had met with a mishap.

Singleton smiled to himself. He particularly wanted Hank and the big 'breed to sweat. As for the one called Ace, the eternally grinning one who had already been killed, he did not spare a single thought about him except once, back when they had been talking to Sam. After that he had simply written Ace off in his thoughts. Ace, and the wounded man called Sam; they would leave Sam to the local law.

It had been distinctly narrowed down. The pair of renegades who were still alive and defiant and deadly, were the ones Singleton had wanted most from the beginning, although until Sam had told him which of the individual renegades had done particular crimes he had not known which were his special enemies.

Now he knew.

Ed Bradley rode into a puny stand of shale-rock oaks, as spindly as though they were no more perhaps than fifty years of age, while in fact they were actually more than a hundred years each. Ed dismounted, loosened the cinch, tied his horse very methodically and shoved back his hat as he moved ahead where he could see eastward, over across the intervening, undulating distance. He had made his judgement by the time Singleton came up and halted at his side.

"Plumb ahead," said the lawman, without looking around at his companion. "This time, we're going to be on the far side of the bastards. That's better'n being between both parties."

Singleton studied landforms then said, "Let's go."

Bradley did not move. "One thing, first," he said. "Back yonder it looked to me like you were going to murder that feller with the busted leg."

Singleton looked at Bradley. "If you got in mind preaching a sermon, don't try it. We've come too far, been through too much. Let's go."

This time it was Ed Bradley following as they walked from the stand of little oak trees.

The land over this far to the west was rougher, with short grass which was already heading out and curing on the stalk, which simply meant the actual earth was very shallow over here, that there was an impervious underlie of hardpan or solid rock, but in either case there was no room for a decent network of roots, so feed came out early over here, and withered or cured with equal haste.

In place there were upthrusts of greyish stone which flaked off under the boots of the walking men. There were increasing indications that this rougher country would improve, would become less liable to have inches deep rock and hardpan the farther Singleton and Bradley walked. Eventually, where they breasted a long-spending rib of rangeland running north and south, they could easily discern the boulder-field, and closer, they could make out two thin stands of trees separating them from the gentle swale where the posse-horses were tied among some scrub-oaks, and some imbedded black boulders which seemed to be some of those house-sized lava boulders which had fallen slightly short of the rock-belt, where most of the boulders had dropped.

Singleton finally swore about their lack of saddleguns and because Bradley had not supported Singleton's suggestion back in town at the livery-barn about getting a couple of Winchesters from the jailhouse-office, he had nothing to say on this score.

They could keep both those onward stands of little trees directly in front of them as they struck out down off their land-swell. From here on, they were in clear danger, not just from being seen as they advanced, but also because, lacking adequate fire-power,

they would be at the mercy of the
outlaws, if they were discovered and
recognised as enemies.

Singleton did not make a sound as
he hiked overland towards the nearest
trees. He was watching dead ahead as
well upon both sides.

The day had been inevitably
wearing along, and somewhere along
the way the sky had begun to fill up
with a metallic variety of shiny
greyness which could presage rainfall, and no one had noticed it. At
least none of them down near that
rock-belt had noticed anything as
unimportant as a slight weather
change.

Singleton and Ed Bradley were
instinctively aware that some of the
glare had left the day, and that some
kind of lethargy-inducing rising
humidity had taken its place, but
they understood this strictly in terms
of perspiration, and otherwise it did
not mean a thing. Particularly as they

got closer and closer to the place where those nervous and fretting tethered horses were partially shaded by oaks and little worthless spindle-pines.

One of the lulls was evidently in progress because there was no gunfire as the pair of stalkers came in from the west. Something else interested Singleton. There was no sign of Hank Foster and his 'breed companion.

It worried Bradley too. He thought they may have given up and departed. Singleton refused to accept this because it would mean another failure, not because it could not be possible. In fact, he had himself pointed out earlier that those renegades had to be utter fools to still be stubbornly pressing this vengeful fight.

Then a solitary rifle opened up, fired off two rounds and went silent again. It had not been fired from over in the rocks, it had been fired from south of the posse-horses where a wide, deep swale bisected the north-south countryside.

Singleton angled slightly in that fresh direction. Bradley followed. They eventually had to abandon the bosque up where the tied horses stood, but neither of them hesitated about this.

Sweat was running under Singleton's shirt and hat. Bradley, who had lost his hat much earlier, had to squint because there was no longer a brim to shield his eyes.

Singleton headed for a waist-high boulder, dropped to one knee over there, shared half the rock with his companion, and waited.

There was no gunfire from either the renegades or the possemen. Singleton ran an appraising glance along the lip of yonder land where the outlaws were, and turned with an enquiring glance to his companion.

Bradley also studied the rim dead

ahead. Once they got up there, they
would probably be able to see the
outlaws across the swale upon the
near side of the far lift and rise.

With luck, they would see Foster
and Juniper before they were themselves seen, which was fine. But the
identical difficulty would still obtain.
They had sixguns of very limited
range. The renegades had Winchesters with a much greater range.

Singleton said, "Constable, by
rights you'd ought to have to jump up
and holler to draw their fire."

Bradley's eyes popped wide open.
"Why?"

"Because you got us out here
without saddle-guns."

Bradley pulled a grass-stalk, bit
down on it and after a moment said,
"Tell you what, Mister Singleton. I'll
got up the slope from here while you
slip around to the north. And when I
figure you're in place and close
enough, I'll bawl like a bay steer so's

they whip around in my direction." Bradley eyed Singleton speculatively, chewing his grass-stalk. "Can you get up along the rim and east without being seen—get close enough to hit someone with a Colt?"

Instead of answering Singleton turned and started away. He could not have answered the lawman's question in any case until he was up near the top of the land-swell where he would be able to see Foster and the 'breed.

That utter stillness with its increasing, weighty humidity which normally accompanied weather changes this time of year, became increasingly noticeable to everyone but Singleton and Bradley.

By the time Singleton was near the edge of the swale his shirt-front was dark and he had to twice mop sweat from his forehead with a limp sleeve, but he still did not raise his eyes.

He halted, waited a moment until his breathing came easier, then dropped down and crab-crawled the final hundred feet.

At the top-out he removed his hat just as a delightful little cooling breeze swept low from north to south. It made his entire head feel ten degrees cooler. He inched up, got prone in the grass and hitched himself the final dozen feet.

The swale down below was wider than most, and it was certainly wider than he had expected it to be. On a cross, like a pair of scarecrows pinned to the ground in the distance, lay Foster and Juniper. Much too far for a Colt and in fact just about too far for even a saddle-gun. They did not look much larger than children.

They were just under the opposite rim, lying in wait, evidently. They had a canteen between them. Otherwise Singleton could not make out any particular details.

He swung slightly to study the land-forms to his left, which would be the direction he must crawl now to get close enough.

There was not a tree, not a rock, not even very much tall grass nor underbrush! Singleton shook off sweat, resettled his hat, decided he had to take chances whether he wanted to or not, and belly-crawled in the grass in the direction of the nearest chaparral thicket.

He was between the tethered horses and the renegades, with another hundred and more yards to go before he could reach the next clump of sheltering underbrush. He did not believe he could get over there without being detected in the attempt.

He lay and sweated, and for the first time began to feel thirsty.

Then an event occurred which probably saved his life. The posse-horses nickered; they were no doubt also thirsty, as well as hungry. They had been tethered all day.

At once Foster and the 'breed

swung to peer north-westerly, evidently suspicious that someone from the rocks may have tried to stalk forward to the horses. Suddenly Tom Juniper pushed back down the slope a few yards, then got to his feet, Winchester carried loosely, and broke over into a long-legged trot heading for the horses—and also heading directly towards the clump of underbrush where Singleton was lying, watching now and scarcely daring to breathe.

16

SINGLETON'S OPINIONS

The situation was fluid. Singleton remained belly-flat and watchful. He expected Ed Bradley to fire off a round or two any moment. The big 'breed was still coming toward him and farther back Foster was watching his companion's progress.

Singleton's danger was acute but he had little time to dwell upon this. There were too many other events occurring. It crossed his mind that if he and Ed could have anticipated any of this, Ed could have crawled around in the opposite direction and with luck might have got upon the other side of Hank Foster.

It was just an idea, and regardless of what its chances were, it was now too late for any of them to inaugurate fresh activity. Each was committed to what he was now doing.

That horse which had nickered was silent, and Singleton presumed the 'breed could see beyond him over where the animals were tied. He could have looked over there, too, but the horses posed no threat to him and the big 'breed did, so he kept his eyes forward.

He began to hope with considerable fervour that Ed Bradley would not fire. At least not until the 'breed was much closer, was close enough so that Singleton would have him in range when the showdown arrived.

Bradley was no doubt watching from low in the grass near the rearward ridge. If so he could scarcely avoid a conclusion about what his part should be now that the circumstances were altered. Singleton hoped very hard this would be the case, and after a while he almost began to relax because although Ed had had plenty of time to fire off a few rounds in accordance with their plan, he did not now do so.

Hank Foster, in Singleton's opinion, was fairly distant to take much of a part in the upcoming shoot-out between his 'breed companion and Singleton, but no doubt he would buy in. If the 'breed went down Foster would be the only one left. He would be a very desperate man.

The 'breed halted, suddenly looking to his left, over in the direction where Singleton had left Ed Bradley. He may have detected movement from the corner of his eye.

Singleton held his breath. The 'breed was still out of hand-gun range. In fact if the 'breed suddenly decided something was wrong and turned back, Singleton could not stop him from doing it.

He stood poised to flee or fight for about five seconds before moving again. Singleton let his breath out slowly. The 'breed still occasionally looked off to his left, so whatever he had seen or *thought* he had seen, was probably tangible enough, but now he was coming with more caution and less haste, and when he finally passed into hand-gun range, he was beyond the point of return. Singleton cocked the Colt, pressed flatter into his cover, and counted the yards separating them. When he was satisfied he could reach out that far, he put down the Colt, wiped sweat from his palm on a trouserleg, picked the gun up and re-gripped it solidly. He was ready.

One final glance back where Hank Foster had returned to his other vigil, the one over towards the rock-belt, another brief look in the direction where he had left Ed, and Singleton was ready.

Tom Juniper slackened his trotting gait slightly as he got almost within sight of the tethered and restless horses. In fact he was looking over the landforms with his head elevated a little to make out each horse back yonder upon the far side of Singleton, and did not look down.

Without warning Singleton rose up out of the grass to one knee, concentrating on his gun and his target. He came up soundlessly and fluidly so that when Tom Juniper dropped his dark stare he was for a fraction of a second immobilised by disbelief, then the Winchester flashed upwards with almost the speed of light as though possessing a heart and brain of its own. The big 'breed had it in both hands swivelling with his entire body to bring the weapon to bear, when Singleton aimed low and fired. The explosion sounded triply loud in all that silence, and cupped as it was into the bowl-like fold of ground.

Singleton had no time to look elsewhere or he would have seen that spring-steel eruption over where Foster was lying as the chief renegade came to his feet gun swinging.

All Singleton was watching was Juniper. The 'breed was hit with solid force, like a mule-kick. He tried desperately to bring the Winchester to bear, but impact had twisted his body half away.

Singleton fired again. That time Juniper lost his carbine, lost his balance and threw out both hands to break his fall. He hung on all fours like a gutshot bear, head slowly drooping.

From a considerable distance a Winchester opened up with its high, waspish sound. Singleton ignored it although he heard it and appreciated that he was being fired upon by Hank Foster. He did not wonder about Ed

Bradley either. He had never before seen a man acting the way Tom Juniper was, beginning to weave from side to side exactly the way a dying bear would have done, refusing to allow either his legs or arms to turn loose because he instinctively knew that the moment he dropped he would never again rise.

Singleton arose, cocked gun extended, and went over there. Foster fired twice very swiftly and Singleton did not even hear the slugs, so evidently they were not very close.

Juniper did not seem to realise he was not alone when Singleton reached and flung the 'breed's holstered Colt over his shoulder. He eased off the hammer of his own weapon, holstered it and leaned to shove the 'breed sideways. That was all it took to up-end Juniper. He fell and twisted to look upwards out of eyes made opaque, almost unseeing, with shock. He had been hit twice and while he might conceivably survive the first, low shot, the second bullet had punctured his upper body from front to back, and whether he felt pain or not, he had to be bleeding-out internally.

That was the bullet wound he would not survive.

From the far distance those carbine shots stopped. Silence settled. Over in the rock-belt there was not a sound and back where the tethered posse-horses were, additional silence drew out and lingered.

Singleton raised his head looking left and right for sign of Ed Bradley, saw nothing, and looked at the man in the grass at his feet.

Juniper was staring, his gaze focusing on something just beyond Singleton, but gradually it came round and settled upon the other man's face. Juniper said, "You double-crossing bastard," in a hoarse tone of voice. "You lousy double-crossing …"

"Save it," exclaimed Singleton going down upon one knee. "I didn't double-cross any of you. I've been on your trail since you bushwhacked the Arapahoes. Since you killed the woman in the tipi. Since Foster shot the little girl in the back of the head."

Juniper continued to stare. He had not until this moment thought there could possibly be that kind of a connection between the man who had shot him and those Indians he had been certain no one even knew about, yet.

He made a circuit of his lips with a sluggish tongue. He looked to Singleton like someone who was growing very tired, very sleepy. He said, "Nothin' but blanket In'ians."

Singleton did not respond to that. He said, "If you know any prayers now'd be a good time to say them."

Juniper's unblinking dry stare did

not waver. "Hank'll kill you, you lousy double-crosser."

Singleton saw the shadow coming, saw the way the big 'breed's expression smoothed out, turned soft and almost gentle. Singleton quietly said, "Good luck," and when Juniper's head dropped, Singleton reached quickly to ease the dead man down slowly.

From a great distance a man's high call echoed and re-echoed. Singleton was slow looking up. He had settled for the Arapahoe woman. Others had settled for the man. There was still one more man to be reckoned with and he expected that shout to signify something pertinent, but there was no one in sight, not even where Foster had been. He was entirely along out there with the dead 'breed.

If that cry had indeed meant something which Singleton would be involved with, at the moment he had no inkling of it. Then he heard another yell, behind him, and turned to watch a rider coming towards him leading a saddled horse. He stepped ten feet away, scooped up the dead renegade's Winchester, levered up a fresh load and waited. The on-coming man called ahead, louder and more urgently this time.

"Hold it! This here is your horse! I'm Paul Dakin from town, one of Sheriff Flannery's possemen. Just keep the gun pointed away from me!"

Singleton waited until he recognised the horse he had been riding, then eased off and grounded the carbine. When the possemen came up, looking tense and spooked, he stared for a long time at the big dead 'breed, then he leaned to hand over the reins to the livery horse and shake his head.

"You two fellers sure got guts to stalk 'em like you done."

Singleton was not interested. He said, "Did you see the other one—

there was another one over along that yonder slope up near the lip."

"Saw him," stated Paul Dakin, without offering to dismount while they conversed. "Yeah, I saw him. And your partner the lawman from Cutbank." Dakin pointed. "Yonder down the far side of the slope." He dropped his hand back to the saddle-swell, dropped his gaze back to Singleton's face. "That renegade run down there. They had their horses hid in the bottom of the swale and he was runnin' down there. Your partner shot him head-on." Dakin paused before also saying, "Climb aboard, mister, and I'll take you over there."

Singleton obeyed. They rode at a steady lope down the trough of the nearby swale, up along the easterly slope, across the ridge—and at the bottom of the adjoining arroyo Singleton saw men standing around a sprawled figure in the grass. He turned from Dakin and set his livery horse directly down the hill.

Ed Bradley was leaning on a carbine which he had not had before he had downed Hank Foster. He watched Singleton come up, step off and push through the silent Fletcherville possemen to halt beside the man on the ground.

Ed said, "I was getting around below them when your fight with the 'breed started. This one came over that darned ridge like he was shot out of a cannon, heading for the horses down here. I didn't know for sure which one he was until I yelled and he turned to shoot at me. I shot first." Ed shrugged. "That's all there was to it."

Singleton eyed the corpse a long time before raising his head as that very erect and hawkish-faced sheriff from Fletcherville returned from conversing with two of his men.

The sheriff strode over, looked

briefly down, then raised his frowning face toward Singleton. "You took unnecessary chances," he said coldly, and Singleton looked steadily at the older man for a moment, cold anger rising.

"You son of a bitch," he said bleakly. "Give me half a chance and I'll ..."

"Hold it," exclaimed a dark-headed big man, thrusting between Singleton and the lawman. "Who the hell do you think you're talking to, cowboy!"

Singleton faced the large dark-headed man. "I was talking to that conceited four-flusher behind you, mister. He deliberately let those renegades get away. He deliberately held off and darn near got me killed. Then he led you fellers into those rocks—without leavin' anyone to mind your horses. Mister, as far as I'm concerned ... !"

"That's enough," exclaimed Ed

Bradley, also pushing forward to step in front of Singleton. "It's done with. If you got the 'breed, that's the end of it." He turned. "Sheriff ... ?"

Flannery glared. "Take those damned horses and clear out of my territory, Bradley, and don't return if you've got *him* with you!"

Singleton stood his ground, gazing steadily at Houston Flannery, contempt in every line of his being. He shook his head, finally, and turned back to his livery horse. Without another word he and the constable from Cutbank got astride and rode away from all those totally silent men down there.

When they reached the ridge again, heading back in the same westerly direction from which they had come to get over this far, Ed said, "You were right. You were right as rain, but if the folks down here think Flannery's so great, why then he's their burden not ours ... Those 'Rapahoe horses and old Hudspeth's animals are back a mile or so, grazing loose."

17

HEADING NORTH

They had no difficulty picking up the loose-stock, which had after all long since become accustomed to being driven, and when they were close enough to Fletcherville to make out people coming over to the west side of town to watch as they loped up, a half or three-quarters of a mile out, Singleton said, "My horse is gone."

Ed looked over where the carcass had been. "Your outfit'll be at the liverybarn."

They left their loose-stock to graze and loped to town leading a pair of the Arapahoe animals. At the back-lot of the liverybarn they swung off to free the livery animals and to rig out the horses they would ride up-country upon.

The hostler came forth to watch, but he did not offer to come close nor to engage them in talk, and as a few additional townsmen walked down through the barn's runway to also stand back and gravely watch, they too preferred not to interfere nor to start a conversation.

When the men from Cutbank were ready they mounted fresh animals, left the livery-horses in a corral, and headed back out where their little remuda was waiting. Singleton was back astride his own saddle, reclaimed from the harness-room back yonder, and he was silent about the horse he had been forced to sacrifice back there, until they had their loose-stock heading forward in a swinging long lope, then he called over to Bradley.

"I should have taken that darned

livery animal. They sure owed me at least that much."

Bradley did not dispute what was owed, but he dryly commented upon another aspect of that scheme. "That sheriff of theirs would have been after us like the devil after a couple of crippled saints, and he'd make it stick if he could catch us in his own territory. That would be horse-stealin'."

Singleton still looked unconvinced so Ed also said, "You got five Arapahoe horses. That's a decent trade for the horse you lost ... My guess is that the In'ians would agree you should have their livestock. Wherever they are, they sure as hell don't need 'em ... Well; at least as far as anyone *knows*, they don't need 'em."

It was a good trail, well marked, and until the rain began to fall they made good time and had no particular difficulties. Afterwards, since neither man had a slicker along, they busted out their remuda in order to make it into the nearest foothill stand of timber. Up there, they continued onward, paralleling the coach-road without going down upon it, protected most of the way from the rainfall, which was not actually hard nor especially heavy, although it continued throughout most of the day.

When the sky opened up a little, showing traces of clear blue, the downpour diminished. By late in the afternoon the sun was shining, the trees continued to drip, and would in fact do so for several hours yet, but Singleton and Bradley had by that time angled their loose-stock over to the roadway, out away from the trees, and pushed steadily onward.

They made an early camp upon a wide, grassy meadow where the horses could fan out and graze. There was little danger of the animals trying to cut back. Horses were never as obnoxious about this as were cattle. Also, horses were usually more wary in the mountains, would not go near dark ranks of trees after nightfall, and could be relied upon to contentedly rest and eat.

Ed fished forth tins of sardines and tossed two over and kept two for himself. "One's for breakfast," he told Singleton, dumped back his hat, up-ended the saddle for something to lean against, and went to work opening the tin in his lap.

"Tell me something," he said, without looking up. "When we get back—what you got in mind?"

Singleton had nothing in mind. He'd only had in mind meeting the Arapahoes and maybe spending a pleasant, lazy summer with them. Now that they were gone, and now that he had done what he'd felt obliged to do to avenge them, his mind was as empty of plans as it had ever been.

"Head back to the south desert," he told Bradley. "This isn't my country. It's beautiful and all, with water and timber and plenty of feed—but I'm desert-raised. I'll go back south as soon as I've helped you get those stock-horses back to the old cowman."

Bradley raised his eyes. "There's work in the Cutbank country, if you need some," he said. "In fact the old gent who owns those cow-horses ..."

"No thanks. I'll head south." Singleton rolled a smoke after eating his first tin of sardines, leaned to get comfortable, then said, "I reckon you're about the only person I can talk to about what happened up here, with me ... I wanted to kill Foster."

Constable Bradley nodded a little. "I figured you did—but it didn't work out that way."

"You didn't let me finish," stated Singleton. "I wanted to kill that bastard right up until I was standing

there looking down at him. Then I
had a feeling ... I got to tell you, Ed,
I was never so relieved about anything in my life. He was paid off, and
I hadn't done it ... You understand?
I wanted to kill all of them for what
they did to those 'Rapahoes, and I
didn't like feelin' that way. It sort of
worried me ... Then I shot the 'breed
and watched him die, and by gawd it
was sort of sickening, so when I went
on down there and saw Foster ..."

Bradley understood. "Couple years
back I had the same feeling about an
outlaw who raided a little ranch east
of Cutbank and deliberately killed
the man of the family. No reason,
just shot him down in cold blood. I
wanted that son of a bitch, and I run
him down and killed him ... I know
the feeling you're talkin' about,
Singleton." Bradley smiled. "Well
hell; it's over with ... You figure to
ever come back up to this country? If

you do—look me up. I'll be glad to see you."

Singleton smiled his first genuine smile in a very long while, then he unrolled his blanketroll willing to sleep without having troubled dreams. It was over. The whole blessed affair was over, and he was tremendously relieved about that. Now, he could get back to loafing away this summer, something he'd been trying to do even before he'd encountered the Arapahoes.